# THE CHAUVINIST

## and other stories

D1611927

# TOSHIO MORI

## Introduction by Hisaye Yamamoto

ASIAN AMERICAN STUDIES CENTER
UNIVERSITY OF CALIFORNIA, LOS ANGELES

Library of Congress Catalog Number: 79–52265
ISBN No. 0–934052–01–8

Asian American Studies Center
Resource Development and Publications
University of California, Los Angeles 90024

Grateful acknowledgment is made to:

*Amerasia Journal*, vol. 3 no. 2, 1976, for permission to reprint "The Chauvinist," by Toshio Mori. Copyright © 1976 by The Regents, University of California at Los Angeles.

*Pacific Citizen* for permission to reprint "Operator, Operator!" "Miss Butterfly," "Japanese Hamlet," and "The Man with Bulging Pockets" by Toshio Mori.

*The Writer's Forum* for permission to reprint "Oakland, September 17" by Toshio Mori. Copyright © 1941 by *The Antioch Press*.

*Hokubei Mainichi* for permission to reprint "The Loser" by Toshio Mori. Copyright © 1955 by *Hokubei Mainichi*.

"1, 2, 3, 4, Who Are We For?" by Toshio Mori was originally printed in *The Clipper*, 1940.

"The Sweet Potato" by Toshio Mori was originally printed in *Current Life*, 1941.

"Between You and Me" by Toshio Mori was originally printed in *Iconograph*.

"The Travelers" by Toshio Mori was originally printed in *All Aboard*, 1944.

# Contents

# Preface

*The Chauvinist and Other Stories* is the second book of short stories published by a Japanese American writer in the United States in thirty years. The first book was *Yokohama, California*, also by Toshio Mori, published in 1949.

Born in Oakland, California in 1910, Toshio Mori is one of the foremost chroniclers of the Japanese American community. During the past forty years, he has written hundreds of short stories and essays, along with several novels. His writings span time and space, from the crowded flower nurseries of San Leandro, California in the 1930s through the bleak World War II concentration camp barracks of Topaz, Utah, to the present.

With wit and compassion, Toshio Mori has illuminated for us the callings and visions of gardeners, housewives, artists, students, and shopkeepers who are among his closest neighbors. Mori's works give meaning to the daily aspirations, struggles, and joys of ordinary people. In this collection of short stories, many are published here for the first time.

This collection would not have been realized without the support and assistance of former and present members of the UCLA Asian American Studies Center. We are indebted especially to Emma Gee, who first saw the need for such a book. Gratitude is also due to Harry Honda of the *Pacific Citizen* and Howard Imazeki of the *Hokubei Mainichi* for giving us permission to reprint several of Mori's stories.

We would like to acknowledge Ron Hirano and Marlon Hom, who took time from their busy schedules and gave freely of their critical advice and humor. This volume could not have been assembled without the aid of Jean Yip, who typed and proofread the manuscript. Peter Horikoshi supplied useful bibliographical materials.

To Toshio Mori, we are indebted for allowing us to print his original works, and to the Mori family, in particular Steve Mori, for their aid and hospitality. Finally, we would like to thank Hisaye Yamamoto, the distinguished writer of short stories, essays, and poems, whose sensibility has provided a focus for this book.

Russell C. Leong
Publications Coordinator
Asian American Studies Center, UCLA

**Toshio Mori, 1979**
photo: Steve Mori

# Introduction

TOSHIO MORI, ENTERING on his sixty-ninth year, is the gentlest of human beings. It is a wonderment to meet him and get to know something about him and to realize that he has, as much as anyone else in the public eye, generated his share of controversy.

One fact remains incontrovertible: he is the first and only Japanese American to have had a book of short stories published in this country (The Caxton Printers, 1949). Upon publication, *Yokohama, California*, is reported to have had a good reception. For instance, Lewis Gannett, book critic for the *New York Herald Tribune*, described Toshio Mori's work as "stories of sunlit loneliness."

And William Saroyan, whose meteor was lighting up the U.S. literary and dramatic scene around that time, introduced Mori to the reading public as "probably the most important new writer in the country at the moment." He further praised the Nisei* as "a natural-born writer" who saw "through a human being to the strange, comical, melancholy truth that changes a fool to a great solemn hero."

Today's generation of Asian American critics, however, has tended to overlook this favorable assessment in order to gnash teeth over the fact that Saroyan could not help detecting occasional lapses in the Mori grammar and syntax. Although on the one hand, these young people have welcomed an older Saroyan's praise for the Sansei poet Lawson Inada, they have taken umbrage at the earlier Saroyan observation and vociferously defended Toshio Mori's writing as the authentic expression of Japanese America.

---

*The Japanese American term for the second generation. The immigrant or first generation is called Issei; the third generation is Sansei.

1

Since most of this introduction is about my tender regard for Toshio
Mori as a person and about my admiration for his work, let me make
clear at the outset that I happen not to agree with the young ones on
this one point of language. I think Toshio, just as I, was trying to use
the very best English of which he was capable, and we have both run
aground on occasion. Probably this was because we both spent the
pre-kindergarten years speaking only Japanese, and, in such cases,
*Sprachgefühl* is hard to come by. (Exceptions such as Conrad, Nabokov
and Baldwin, who are born hearing other accents and who later
achieve complete mastery over the King's English, making it do exactly
what they want it to do, are few and far between.) We differ from
someone like Milton Murayama, whose use of pidgin in *All I Asking
for Is My Body* (San Francisco, 1975) is deliberate, studied, whose
use of the English language is otherwise impeccable, or like Momoko
Iko, whose plays are piquantly sprinkled with Japanese phrases, to
good effect.

There has been afoot in recent years a movement for the recognition
of Black English and such. Regional and ethnic influences have given
the language a marvelous variety and vitality. But communication is
the aim of writing, and if there is not some degree of codification,
some rules, so that Chicano English or Nisei English can be identified
for what it is, the reader will flounder. (I remember my first- and last-
attempt to read Joel Chandler Harris, which I guess is neither here
nor there.) And Toshio and I were both trying to follow some older
regulations.

True, the reader may encounter in these stories a homely phrase
which will evoke another time. Wakako Yamauchi, artist and writer,
was delighted to come across the word "snails" in "Operator, Operator!" That was what we used to call cinnamon rolls. In those days,
everything we approved of was "swell," and one's "old man" meant
one's father. Otherwise, there is small attempt to reproduce Japanese
American lingo as such.

The harshest attack on *Yokohama, California* came from a brash
young man at the time, Albert Saijo, who has himself since gone on
to become a writing member of the Beat Generation. Writing in the
Japanese American weekly, *Crossroads*, for March 29, 1949, Saijo
included Mori in a blanket condemnation of all Nisei writing as being
characterized by "muddled intelligence . . . sentimentality . . . and
poor craftsmanship." Even though in the beginning of the diatribe,
Saijo professed to finding "no virtue at all" in Japanese American
literature, his essay eventually got around to discerning "a certain
vigor and charm" in some of the Mori pieces, as well as to the grudging

admission that there were other stories in which "he does manage to convey the Issei character with some truth." In fact, there was almost outright approval of the story called "The Chessmen."

But now, a later generation, hungry for its roots (to attempt to look into the future these days, after all, is to invite vertigo), has embraced Toshio Mori to its bosom. In the wave of militant ethnicity that followed the Watts riots and associated events, and the semi-awakening of a portion of the white majority to the fact that something was rotten, not only in the so-called underdeveloped countries, but right here under its own nose, first the Black, then Chicano and Native American, and then Asian American, in a me-too, domino effect, rediscovered those individuals in their past who had managed somehow to write down their impressions of the world immediately about them. Thus, in Toshio Mori's stories, young Asian Americans have found a precious record of their heritage which few at the time deemed important enough to preserve.

Out of this growing ethnic consciousness emerged the first Asian American Writers' Conference, sponsored at Oakland Museum, by the Combined Asian American Resources Project, (March 1975); the second similar event, the Pacific Northwest Asian American Writers' Conference, sponsored at the University of Washington in Seattle (June 1976); the Talk Story Ethnic Writers' Conference at Mid-Pacific Institute in Honolulu (June 1978). Toshio Mori has been an honored panelist at these and smaller gatherings, and particularly at the Seattle 1976 conference, where younger writers such as Frank Chin and Lawson Inada singled him out for homage as their very own pioneer, telling of their excitement when they first discovered him as a predecessor. This present UCLA collection, which excludes the stories in the *Yokohama* volume, is to be joined by the Bay Area's Isthmus Press edition of a Mori novel, *Woman from Hiroshima*.

Peter Horikoshi, whose taped interview in *Counterpoint* is the source of some of my material, has kindly xeroxed *Yokohama, California* for me. Some of the *Yokohama* stories are available in just about every Asian American anthology extant: *Asian-American Authors* (Boston, 1972), *Aiiieeeee! An Anthology of Asian American Writers* (Washington, D.C., 1974), *Asian-American Heritage* (New York, 1974), the special Asian American issue of *Greenfield Review*, "Asian American Writers Issue" (New York, 1977), *Counterpoint: Perspectives on Asian America* (Los Angeles, 1976), and in both the original and updated editions of *Speaking for Ourselves* (Chicago, 1969), as well as the tenth grade reader, *In Question* (New York, 1975), part of Harcourt Brace Jovanovich's *Variations* textbook series.

Toshio Mori wrote several hundred short stories, out of which Russell Leong and I have considered perhaps sixty and then whittled that number down to the present twenty or so. There is one published Mori novel, *Woman from Hiroshima*, in which the saga of Japanese American life from its beginnings in Japan up to the period after the Second World War is recounted through the voice of an Issei woman speaking to her grandchildren. (Some chapters appeared in the *Pacific Citizen* in the 1950s.) In addition, there are five unpublished novels: "Send These the Homeless," written in camp in 1942, is about evacuation; "The Brothers Murata" (original title, "Peace, Be Still"), which spells out the conflict between two Nisei brothers who are politically on opposite sides in World War II, was completed in 1944. There is also "Way of Life" (working title), which he wrote in the 1960s and which is not about Japanese but about whites during the Depression.

In going over Toshio Mori's work in bulk, in order to help select these few stories, what emerged for me was the panorama of Japanese America in the early 1930s, in the later 30s as the storm clouds gathered, and in the concentration camps of 1942–45, stretched on a canvas from here to there, a veritable Floating World.* No one else has kept this account of our lives, in fiction and in personal essay, in such detail, with such compassion.

## II.

There were some unusual aspects to Toshio Mori's childhood.

His parents both came from the town (it is now a city, Toshio says) of Otake in Hiroshima prefecture. They were married in Japan and had two sons before the father, leaving his family behind, made his way to Hawaii in the late 1800s. He worked for a time on sugar plantations before continuing on to the mainland, arriving in San Francisco in the 1890s (in plenty of time to experience the great earthquake-fire of 1906). Contacting others from his hometown, he bought an Oakland bathhouse from one of them. It was here Toshio was born in 1910, because his mother back in Japan had meanwhile earned her own passage to America by selling fruits and vegetables in the resort

*Translation of *ukiyo-e*, referring to genre pictures and prints, especially of the Edo or Tokugawa period. Best known in the Western world in this field are the names Hokusai (1760–1849) and Hiroshige (1797–1858). I am thinking particularly of the latter, because he is reported to have been the modest one.

town of Miyajima. Around 1912, while still holding on to the bath-house, Toshio's father entered into an Oakland nursery partnership with relatives. About that time, too, the family was joined by the Mori's older sons from Japan, who seemed to Toshio more like uncles than brothers because of the age disparity. Indeed, for a time, he says, he was under the impression that the oldest brother, who subsequently opened a store in Oakland, was his father.

The bathhouse was sold in 1913, the year before the First World War began, in favor of the Oakland nursery. The nursery partnership was dissolved in 1915, and the Mori family moved to San Leandro to begin a nursery farm of their own, and there Toshio Mori has dwelt ever since, amongst the sweet peas, stocks, snapdragons, dahlias and zinnias, except for the wartime years at Tanforan racetrack and Topaz relocation center in Utah.

There was another brother "who died early," as well as the younger brother who, permanently disabled in fighting with the 442nd Regimental Combat Team, has reared his family in the San Leandro area.

Toshio remembers his father as being a silent man who rolled his own Bull Durham and read the Japanese newspaper. He does not remember that his father ever scolded him for anything.

On the other hand, his mother appears to have been the kind of "talk story" mother that Maxine Hong Kingston has commemorated in her brilliant and poetic book, *The Woman Warrior* (New York, 1977) or the Eliza Gant matriarch that Thomas Wolfe is reported to have modeled after his own mother. She figures prominently as the one who discouraged him from taking up professional baseball (Toshio's high school coach had arranged for him to try out with the Chicago Cubs). Perhaps she had had enough of familial separations, but she thought Chicago was too far for her son to go. She encouraged his writing, however, even to the point of commenting that he was doing entirely too much reading to ever write anything. This remark prompted him to give away his books so he could concentrate on writing.

Toshio was born at a time when the American Dream was still providing options for all who believed in it—every boy, for instance, had a chance to become President of the United States. He first took up art in the Oakland schools, later considered becoming a Buddhist missionary, then there was the dream of becoming a big league ball-player, and it was not until he was inspired by his English teacher at Oakland High School, Mary B. Sheridan, who thought a sketch of his "pretty vivid," that he began to think about perhaps becoming a writer. What really clinched his decision, however, was the favoritism shown a classmate who had a flair for writing; he determined then this was a pretty good course to follow. He had the same English teacher for all of his four years at Oakland High.

Toshio also attended Japanese school, as most of us Nisei did. He went every weekday afternoon from four to six, after regular school, to the Buddhist Church which doubled as a language school, from the time he was eight to about his third year in high school. However, he has never visited Japan as some of the younger Asian American writers have made a point of doing (James Masao Mitsui, Garrett Kaoru Hongo, Karen Yamashita, Alan Chong Lau, Alfred Robles, Joy Kogawa) and says he has never had any particular desire to do so.

But the awareness of one's Japanese connections was omnipresent then as now, and some Nisei who gave the matter thought tended to look upon themselves as a bridge between East and West. Particularly in that time of tension in the thirties when Japan began to occupy Manchuria under the eyes of a disapproving world, and Japanese in the United States began to feel some of the backlash on top of the already existing prejudice (I was around ten then, but I remember feeling that I was somehow responsible when the subject was brought up in class, especially when the teacher-principal assigned a composition on the topic, "What I will do if war breaks out between the United States and Japan . . ."), it seemed necessary to begin taking a stand of some kind. Several of Toshio's stories of that period touch on this theme. "The Sweet Potato" and "1,2,3,4, Who Are We For?", both included in this volume, contain references to the awkward Nisei situation.

Dr. Kenneth Yasuda, another older Nisei (b. 1914), whose book of translated and original *haiku*, *A Pepper-pod* (New York, 1947), points up this feeling as he dedicates the book to Basho and Buson "in a hope that a bridge may be built between East and West."

The bridge theme is found elsewhere in Asian American literature, as in the film and book, *Bridge to the Sun* (Chapel Hill, North Carolina, 1957) by Gwen Terasaki, narrating the real-life courtship and marriage of a Japanese diplomat and a young white woman.

Anyway, the idea of such a bridge conjures up in my mind that stunning red wooden structure in the Huntington Gardens in San Marino, California. Its steps arch steeply over a pond of water, and it is roped off, not meant for crossing at all. The notion was commendable, beautiful, but proved unworkable because that was not exactly what those in power in both countries had in mind. The handful of Nisei who did go to Japan found themselves stranded there by the war; some of them eventually discarded the dual citizenship that all Nisei were born with and chose to become Japanese citizens. The most famous strandee was Iva Ikuko Toguri, who only recently, after a prison term and years of ignominy, has been exonerated.

Toshio doesn't seem to have thought much of bridge-building. In "The Sweet Potato," he writes:

> I knew what was coming next. All summer we had argued about our-selves . . . the problem of the second generation of Japanese ancestry. "I tell you. We're not getting anywhere. We haven't got a chance," he would tell me. "We'll fall into our parents' routine life and end there. We'll have our own clique and never get out of it.
>
> "You're wrong, Hiro," I would say. "We'll climb and make ourselves heard. We have something in us to express and we will be heard."

Later on, in the same story, the friend gets insistent again:

> "What do you think? Do you think our people will ever be noticed favorably? What can we Japanese do? Must we accomplish big things here in America?"
>
> "Little things can accomplish big things, too, I think," I said.

Nor did he fall in too closely with other young Nisei who leaned toward radical politics, as was the intellectual fashion in the thirties. Evidently he saw more promise locally than in Russia's reordering of priorities.

## III.

When Toshio was twenty-two years old and working ten to twelve hours almost every day of the week out in the nursery, he once and for all made up his mind to become a writer. From spending his spare time at bookstores and libraries, he knew that Ernest Hemingway and Sherwood Anderson, among others, had made their mark in their twenties. He set himself the rigorous schedule of writing from ten at night until two in the morning, after regular working hours. He says he did not mind the field work because the manual tasks allowed his mind the freedom to roam at will among the ideas and plots he would try to put down on paper after dinner.

He estimates that he collected enough rejection slips "to paper a room." He did not submit his work to the English sections of the Japanese language newspapers of his area, as most Nisei writers of the time did. He has said more than once that he was "a loner," going out of his way to avoid the neighbors in order to have more time for writing. He says Sherwood Anderson's *Winesburg, Ohio* was a great influence on his way of looking at the lives around him (see Dorothy Ritsuko McDonald's unpublished essay: "Toshio Mori: *Yokohama, California* and Sherwood Anderson," 1976).

At first his writing was aimed at the slick magazines, because of the top money paid by such publications, but as he continued to write, his principal output concerned the Issei and Nisei of his acquaintance in and around Oakland and San Leandro. He wrote of these Japanese, he has said, in order to explain Japanese America to the white reading public. We have included in this volume one story which was probably in the "commercial" category, "The Loser," which contains no specific reference to Japanese. However, I once knew an Issei lady who could have posed for Toshio's portrait of "The Loser." It is written with fine irony and is as good as any of de Maupassant.

When Toshio was twenty-eight, he got his first acceptance, from *Coast* magazine, which had been financed by wealthy Californians who wanted a West Coast magazine along the lines of the *New Yorker*. And the fact remains that it wasn't any of us who helped Toshio Mori when he was starting out. That was William Saroyan who saw the story in *Coast*, got in touch with him, went for walks with him, sat over cafe meals with him, all the while expounding an ebullient, infectious view of life. That was Saroyan encouraging him to get more of his work into print.

He also came to the attention of Sanora Babb, wife of cinematographer James Wong Howe, a writer in her own right. (She has transmuted a childhood on the bleak Colorado plains into the finest literature.)

So Toshio Mori, in the 1940–41 period, was already making waves in the literary world, with such magazines as *The Clipper*, *Iconograph*, *Writer's Forum* and *Common Ground* welcoming him as a new and refreshing voice. He was also sought out by his fellow Nisei for contributions to a literary monthly called *Current Life*.

To cap it all, Caxton Printers, of Idaho, then best known for the Vardis Fisher sagas, put Toshio Mori's *Yokohama, California* on its spring 1942 publications list. This was quite an achievement, because publishers are notoriously leery of short story collections.

## IV.

Then came December 7, 1941. The events of that day altered the plans of just about every Japanese living in America, and Toshio Mori's life underwent its share of drastic changes.

For one thing, Caxton Printers decided to shelve *Yokohama* indefinitely. Among the 110,000 Japanese moved out from the Western Defense Command, Toshio and his family were among those who were first sent to Tanforan racetrack in San Bruno before shipment out to one of the nine permanent relocation centers. The Mori family was assigned to Topaz, the Central Utah Relocation Project.

Toshio remembers a sense of desperation at Tanforan, "I felt I would be a prisoner for life." But the dislocation did not stop him from writing. "The Man with the Bulging Pockets," included here, a tragi-comic comment on human nature, is one of the results of his Tanforan stay. Reading it is like watching a drawing come to life from Mine Okubo's *Citizen 13660* (New York, 1978).

In Topaz, assigned to the documentation section, Toshio continued to write. That most serendipitous of all camp publications, *Trek* magazine, came from this chance assembly of several of the top Nisei artists and writers: Mine Okubo, Jimmy Yamada, Taro Katayama, Toyo Suyemoto, others. The first issue of the magazine came out in time for Christmas 1942; *Trek* was to go three memorable issues before most of its editors scattered to points east. Toshio, staying on at Topaz, edited a fourth issue called *All Aboard*, which prodded the dispersion of those remaining. He himself was once sorely tempted to relocate, when a job offer came in from Carl Sandburg, who wanted someone with literary aspirations to come help tend the hogs in Galesburg, Illinois.

Meanwhile, Toshio's younger brother Kazuo, a member of the all-Nisei combat team which trained at Camp Shelby, Mississippi was reported seriously injured on the Italian front. He was later transferred to the veterans' hospital in Auburn, California, a town which had made the news for having refused a haircut to a returning Nisei war veteran. Toshio and his family were given permission to return to San Leandro, where they were able to get the nursery back into shape. Some of this time is recounted in "Unfinished Message," wherein a mother's concern reaches from beyond the grave. I have heard Toshio read this story at least three different times and have gotten chills down my spine every time.

*Yokohama, California* finally came out in 1949, four years after war's end, eight years later than originally announced.

## V.

In both *Yokohama* and the present collection, I find a Zen flavor to several of the stories. It is particularly notable in "Trees" in the *Yokohama* book. In fact, a Buddhist priest in charge of Soto-Zen in San Francisco, the Reverend Takahashi, has told Toshio that he has read the story twenty-seven times!

In "Trees," two friends, Fukushima and Hashimoto, take a turn around the latter's *bonsai* garden. Fukushima repeatedly begs to know the secret of Hashimoto's serenity. Hashimoto's matter-of-fact, eminently sensible answers remind one of the statement of the philosopher George Santayana's mother, who when asked how *she* spent her days, replied, "I try to stay warm in the winter and cool in the summer."

So, although Toshio Mori disclaims any intention of promulgating the attainment of *satori*, he appears to have reached some similar condition himself, looking on the people and events about him with a bemused and tolerant eye. Even of that traumatic time for most of us, the wholesale uprooting, Toshio comments, offhandedly, "I believe it was a social experiment." His is a really sanguine attitude, when you consider that there are many of us clamoring for redress thirty-seven years or so after the fact.

And what of the prejudice that all of us have borne the brunt of, to some degree or other? In Toshio Mori's stories, it is the white who is marginal, only incidentally mentioned if he impinges on our daily lives, but in some of these pieces, we are made aware that he has been out there all the time, writing the rules of the game. Anti-Japanese discrimination in California is a fact of life which Toshio has accepted and taken in stride long since; within the shelter of the Japanese community, dignity has been possible.

The backgrounds of the stories that we have chosen are variegated: there are, naturally, flower shops and nursery fields, there is Treasure Island with its Japanese pavilion and green tea ice cream, Chinatown, Oakland (sometimes called Ashland) and its Japanese ghetto, Tanforan assembly center with its equine smell, Topaz blooming in the middle of the Utah desert, the small town outside Topaz that typifies all the dinky towns that served as arrival and departure stations for the evacuated and the relocating, the veterans' hospital.

And there is more. In this Floating World, despite the specters of depression, war, concentration camps and prejudice, there still appears to be some semblance of order, a sense of purpose. A theme reiterated by several stories is that of the mysterious and unquenchable human spirit accommodating itself to reverses and finding its lights to go on by. There is the Nisei determined to be a Shakespearian actor; there is the Issei who has filled his whole front porch with abalone shells and who still collects more, or who drives his family to distraction by playing lifelong the only *shakuhachi* piece he knows (the song is called "The Distant Call of the Deer"). In "Operator, Operator!" there is the proud and aging Issei, no longer employable, who is kin to the Filipino expatriates in Bienvenido Santos' "The Day the Dancers Came" (*Letters in Exile*, Los Angeles, 1976). The most remarkable story is "The Chauvinist," whose deaf protagonist lives a passionate and lyrical interior life counterpointing the plodding routine of his exterior existence:

Turn the disk of earth: a bed is soaring. The clouds roar. The rivers dry. The skies drop. The sun melts. The man is bigger than the earth. Why? A dream is a better production than Warner Brothers pictures. A dream is the reality in hope; and reality the nightmare of a dream reversed. Destruction and education hand in hand. Red Cross and butchery on the same fields. Death and birth in Ward E. Asylum and earth together: fences. Barefoot and shoes, and nudism and morality. One man and one woman. One man and two women. One woman and two men. One man and many women. One woman and many men. The impatience of man. The patience of man. He sleeps. He wakes. The sleep of a man and the disk of earth continues.

Another group of stories catches the charm and shock of conversations overheard. Toshio's ear is attuned to such situations, especially when Nisei encounter one another fleetingly at a point of departure, as in "Oakland, September 17," when a Nisei girl on the eve of an arranged marriage, a produce truck driver and a nurseryman, strangers to one another, converge at a soda fountain and exchange pleasantries and intimacies.

There are included here four pieces which have to do with the camp experience. In fact, two of them are virtually one and the same story, except that one, "The Long Journey and the Short Ride," is a first-person account, and the other, "The Travelers," is a fictionalized version of the same happening. We thus get a glimpse into how one author at least shapes the raw dough of fact into the nicely-browned loaf of fiction.

Then there are some selections which enable us to look into Japanese American home life. We watch as two young sisters obligingly get into formal kimonos to perform dances for an old friend of their father who has been overcome with nostalgia for Japan. We follow a kid who, behind his father's back, goes through a breathless, hectic day trying to go into the florist business for himself, in competition with his father. We wonder what has really happened at a neighboring house, from where there has evidently been the abrupt departure of the oldest son, while the family, out of Ibsen, continues its outward routine as though nothing untoward has taken place.

Finally, there are a couple of stories which do not exactly fall into any category. "My Uncle in the Philippines" recounts the legend of an uncle who was the black sheep of the family, who fumbled a promising military career and disappeared into the boondocks. In "Four-Bits," we go along in curiosity and embarrassment with a bunch of fellows to a cafe where a former classmate of theirs has been discovered to be earning her living as an ecdysiast.

What moves me the most about these stories is the people, especially those who exemplify the bulldog tenacity of the human spirit. Toshio has no doubt been well aware of the fact that such stories also constitute an apology for the writer's own life, for his persistence in continuing to write despite the odds. "The Confessions of an Unknown Writer" shares with us the bitter melon taste of the discouragement that Toshio must have indulged in from time to time.

In this connection, I am put in mind of a couple of other Californians who built their own monuments, Simon Rodia, sculptor of the Watts Towers, and Baldasare Forestiere, who built a ten-acre underground mansion in Fresno. Rodia, tilesetter, created over a period of thirty-three years those three marvelous Cambodian temples which spiral heavenwards almost one hundred feet. He worked with whatever came to hand: bedsprings, bits of bottle glass, fragmented tiles, broken dishes, chunks of rock, all cemented and reinforced with scrounged steel and wire. Forestiere, former subway worker, went in the opposite direction, excavating for forty years to produce over one hundred underground chambers, courtyards, passageways, patios, grottos, a chapel and a large auditorium, all with the appropriate furnishings. He even planted several different kinds of citrus trees, each growing towards its own skylight. Toshio Mori seems to me to have come from the same mold. He has built his monument, however, with intangibles: observation, meditation, bits of conversation; snatches of Shakespeare, rumors from Japan, the iridescence of abalone shells, the poignant wail of a wooden flute, the whiff of hot doughnuts; trees growing, flowers blooming, these faithful descriptions of men, women and children caught in the act of living.

## VI.

Naturally, Toshio Mori has been asked more than once whether, if he had the choice, he would do it again. He answers yes. His health held up okay under the arduous writing regimen of the early years. Only once did he have doubts about his stamina. This was one day when he had the alarming sensation that his heart had burst. Otherwise, he has continued to write in good health, even while making a living in public relations after the war. But there is one clue to the rigors of his writing life. He confesses he felt dismay on learning that his only son was following in his footsteps (Stephen Mori has been making a name for himself as a photo-journalist). One gathers that he would have wished for him, as all we parents do for our children, an easier vocation.

Thus, Toshio Mori is a survivor in a craft which is famous for killing off its practitioners at an early age or slowly destroying them. In the last couple of years, Asian American literature has had a couple of tragic casualties (David Hsin-fu Wand, Bayani Mariano). It was Edmund Wilson who observed that most of his contemporaries had either gone mad, committed suicide or become Roman Catholics. Toshio Mori chose none of the above, and his writing indicates it was because, whether he was conscious of it or not, he had gradually arrived at his private brand of enlightenment. While I tend to be from Missouri on such subjects as extra-sensory perception, after-life phenomena, unidentified flying objects, et cetera, my mind is not closed to the possibility of such phenomena, and it has occurred to me that the episode of the heartburst, otherwise unexplained, may have signalled some sort of psychic breakthrough. (I have heard a man, whose word I have no reason to doubt and who has led an extraordinary life, describe the appearance of a "blue flame" in his room one night.)

In "1936," Toshio Mori's exultant statement about the wonder of life, he said about his dentist friend:

It is like a moth flying towards the red hot lamp, myself leaping kangaroo-like to shake hands and derive some good and warmth from this man, an alive one.

And:

All this will be forgotten . . . how at one time such and such a thing happened and that there ever was a writer for its days, and that the people of 1936 [were] once living.

That was over forty years ago. But none of it has been forgotten because Toshio Mori, an alive one, issue of migrants from a small Asian archipelago, has gone out of his way to tap them out for us on sheets of tree pulp, using hieroglyphics which originally arrived here by slow boat from the European continent. That this has made him, indisputably, the pioneer of Japanese American literature is like one of the felicities in his own short stories.

—Hisaye Yamamoto

*Ed. note:* Ms. Yamamoto has published works in *Partisan Review*, *Kenyon Review*, and *Harper's Bazaar*, among others, and for the last twenty-five years, has contributed essays and poems to the *Rafu Shimpo*.

# I
# CALLINGS NEAR AND FAR

# The Chauvinist

KETTLE WHISTLES. THREE pans of corn boil. Tall glasses tinkle with the touch of human hands. Plates rattle and scratch one another. An ancient refrigerator rumbles every once in a while. A clock on the wall ticks time, and he whistles a tune that was once the rage a few months ago. Voices in the living room murmur like a chorus in a classical work. An electric mixer whirls. Result: mayonnaise for tuna salad. Cheese crackers crackle coming out of a two-pound carton. Knives, forks, and spoons contact the forks, spoons, and knives; and the melody of the kitchen ensues.

He's a man on Ninth Street with a great calling. A calling that may some day replace priests and theology. A calling demanding dignity, humbleness, humor, and the limits of human traits. The sadness of this particular man's role is that it must be kept a secret. He couldn't go out in the street and shout with all the might of his lungs just what he's doing as a contribution toward the harmony of human beings. He isn't looking for immortality; so he denounces personal immortality. He is looking for immortality of the man living today who is to die tomorrow. Call it as he does: Everyday immortality.

Takanoshin Sakoda has been at it for a long time. In his quiet solemn way he's been searching among his friends and people the solution to his school of thoughts. He isn't extraordinary. He isn't brilliant, and inside his head there isn't a bag full of philosophical ideas or tricks. There isn't a particle of outstanding skill in him which may be the undoing of his calling. There is just one thing which sets him apart from the rest of men and that's the story hereon.

People look and size him up: When he talks he is like a swirling river seeking an ocean outlet. He won't hear other people's words. He just goes on talking. He forgets the people, the background, and even himself to the point of nothingness in a subject of temporary importance.

Friends look at him from another angle: Lucky guy. Stone deaf. Doesn't have to plug cotton in his ears when to bed he goes with little wifey. Doesn't need to pick up little issues of a family circle. The innocent among the snoopy gossipers and savages of dirty insults. The babe in the gusty screechy roar of modern mads—the genius of the community due to an accidental lack of a sense.

The family in one voice (wife, daughter, and son): The blessed wit. One-half of a battleless ground. The desert of mind, culture, age, and ambition. The portrait of a man in a thousand years: a "houseband"—the meek follower of a new sufferage for power (now) and beauty (in future). The seed of a new vogue: the specialist specializing with a lack of one human sense or more. Examples of possibilities: the blind artist painting on the accepted presence of a canvas; the deaf musician composing a fresh score—new tones, new scales, new instruments; the tongueless chef concocting a new dish fit for a connoisseur; the mouthless moralist discovering in silence the language of expression; the average man on earth smelling the presence of man on Mars.

Today is the day. Takanoshin is sitting in the kitchen having finished his duties early. Everything's cooked; everything's on the table ready to be guzzled by the ladies. The women arrive. It's seven in the evening, and his wife hasn't returned. Business must've been good. Good business on Monday. Monday is Community Women's Club night.

Mrs. Tamada is looking at him and addressing Mrs. Abe. "Sometimes I believe he can hear us," she is saying. "Sometimes I see an intelligent look on his face as if he knows everything that's going on."

"Nonsense!" Mrs. Abe replies. "Look at him! Unless he's a good actor, and I know he isn't, he couldn't stare at us so long with that empty blandness of his without being genuine."

Mrs. Tamada is dubious of her companion's words. "Sometimes I feel he's laughing at us."

"Here, here! What's all this debating about?" Mrs. Tariki cuts in.

Mrs. Tamada and Mrs. Abe turn their backs on Takanoshin. "We're talking about Takanoshin. Tamada-*san* says he's very intelligent and can see through us," Mrs. Abe says.

"I did not!" Mrs. Tamada says.

Mrs. Tariki laughs. It's time to put everyone in place. It's about time someone definitely define the activity of Takanoshin. "Picture him sitting there night after night waiting for his wife and worrying about supper getting cold," she says. "Picture him with an apron housecleaning twice a week while his wife and daughter run the grocery store."

"He's lazy, weak, and boneless," Mrs. Abe says.

"He should be ashamed of himself staying home by the warm stove while his wife is working at the store," adds Mrs. Tamada.

The fourth woman enters the conversation. "The weasel. The tramp. The mind of a monkey," Mrs. Miyakawa says. "Good for nothing."

The four women turn and look in Takanoshin's direction.

He is nonchalantly sitting in the corner, the way immobile and wise people do. He meets their glances with a smile, the way the tolerant sages of history should have done. He is all smiles because he could not have heard the conversation. He is deaf. His ears are out of order. He looks at the ceiling and smiles. Everything is out of order. The arrangement of his life for instance is out of order. The women are out of order; his family is out of order. The system of civilization is out of order. Ditto the people and the world.

Out of his isolation in the kitchen (cooking three meals a day is his relation to the labor problem today) he has discovered one of the biggest scoops of scientific nature. It took him eighty days and nights to see the light that one of the biggest things out of order on earth is the facts misarranged. The facts of life are; the past thus, the future thus. Proven with dignity and pomp; prophesized with sanity and bearing it is to laugh. Tonight two stars have fallen. I saw two of them fall while I was outdoors for a bit of night air. That's the fact of life for today and another day. It was time that one man on Eighth Street in the year 1939 come to grief. It was once simple to prove the fact of an event. The world in general is concerned over me because I am deaf. Even at this moment when I am sitting here peacefully and listening to the conversation as sanely and conscious as the women themselves, I am proof of the deaf living.

I the man who remains silent to the little voices about me. I did not declare myself to be anything. I am one of the living proofs of a fact purported to life. One day I simply sat down, and the family began to screech at me. It took them ten minutes to come to my side and look at each other's faces. "He can't hear," my son hoarsely whispers. "He's gone deaf!" my daughter screams. My wife pales and begins to sway and the children rush her to the sofa. Commotion arose. People came in and out. Doctors looked over me. I became the attraction of the community.

Although the news of myself being deaf became old and died, I myself knew no better than to become the beginning of a new refreshment of life. I endorse myself, my life, to the young mind—not for mischief and trouble making. I address to the suppressed, the futile, the jobless, the woman's husband, the lonely hearts. I also address the romanticist—here is something in your line. I am deaf. This is untruth but I'm not lying. A liar is a cheat who harms others. I am like a beggar who must become blind to make a living. The only difference is that I have become deaf to survive the living. The world is waiting for a new philosophy. This is the age for science and invention. People deride the experimenters' failures but we need the experimenters and the failures. We need them just as we need the untruths. Truth without untruth, it's false. By representing the truth in untruth and untruth in truth I may become someone I want to be.

Mrs. Sakoda returns home. The women stand. The meeting begins right away. Tonight is the flower arrangement night. Refreshments are served. Mrs. Sakoda is speaking, "My, he's ruined the punch again!"

"Mama! Will you taste the salad! It's salty!" the daughter calls from the next room.

The women look at Takanoshin sitting in the adjoining room and laugh. They laugh heartily and the words are heard through the house.

"I'm sorry, girls," Mrs. Sakoda is speaking again. "The evening's spoiled again. I've told him over and over and he comes right back and does the same thing again."

Pretty soon their men will be coming around to take them home. They will park their cars at the front and blow their horns. The women run out to the door and call them in. The coffee is served. The conversation is now general. The men talk of business and fishing and club activities. The art of flower arrangement is over. With the entry of each man, the men perk up and smile. The weather is fine these days. Business is good. How's yours? My car goes sixteen miles on a gallon. I caught a fifteen pounder. A striped bass near Antioch. My luck's been bad. A cop pinched me in the city. Yeah, a fine. My house needs painting. Business is so bad I put it off every year. Why don't you run up to my brother's place in San Jose? He'll be glad to see you after all these years. Why don't you? Thanks. I don't know. Oh, go ahead.

Do these men talk this way away from here? Do they in their privacy speak in such a milky language? I wonder if their thoughts run parallel to the mere words of their lips. I wonder if they are dead so soon. They talk in the same tone, same gestures, same subject, same hobbies, same duties and obligations, same destiny. Why doesn't someone talk about death (slow death) some night? The death in the flower arrangement. The death in the flower. The death in our life. The death of a birth. Some people wouldn't glibly talk; it would take their minds off talk. And the silence would be refreshing and strange. Imagine the silence at the women's club meeting. The silence in a deaf man's house. The silence wouldn't be eternal; make no mistake about that. It wouldn't be what we would like to have but ah, what is eternal? And at this moment the records of Beethoven, Sibelius, Ravel, Gershwin stop. The great poems end, Shakespeare included. The books of Tolstoy, Joyce, Whitman, Emerson, Tagore; and what have you left?

I would sit for an answer by the shore and watch the waves come in. I would lie on the hills and watch the sun for awhile. The clouds a good deal longer. I would go to the river side and watch the boats sail the waters; the trains dash by; the airliners roar overhead.

It isn't there, an early observer tells the younger generation. It isn't there. Look somewhere else. At last the young generation claim. It isn't here. It isn't nature. It isn't man's civilization or man's heredity or his environment. It isn't man's possessions or capabilities, the younger generation point. It's his possibilities that count. It's a shame to see the simplicity of each generation. This is so, that is so, all is so. The man's thoughts are the seeds of the future. The last region of man is sleep, next to nothingness. The sleep of man awake. The sleep of man sleeping. The sleep of man dreaming. The sleep of man dead. The sleep of man in birth.

The night is over. The women leave. The men follow. Goodbye, Abe-*san*. Goodnight, Tamada-san. Goodnight, Miyakawa, Yamamoto, Hama, Suzuki. See you next Monday. Tea ceremony next time. Oh, let's drag Karita-*san* next time. Smiles. More smiles. Handshakes. Hand waves. Brave smiles. Sad faces at departure.

The night is over for them. The night is dead. And sleep is a period between sunset and sunrise. The saddest of faces is the man or woman too lonely to be alone. The loneliest hour is the time before sleep and the awakening of conscious motor after sleep.

A man's loneliness is an offshoot of the women's club meeting every Monday night. The crowd which the theaters draw isn't due to the attraction of the picture or the stars, but the vacuum emptiness in each individual's search for the solace. A song like "Donkey's Serenade" takes hold of the audience. It is trivial and full of death, but we are impressed temporarily. Everything we touch is full of death and triviality.

And when we sense something like a poem or a symphony or a painting that would not die we are surprised. It makes us forget temporarily by reaching out for something permanent and enduring. And often when we return to ourselves our life is like the song "Donkey Serenade" (full of death and short life)—the actuality of our faces, our houses, our cars, our relatives, our bank accounts.

"Papa-*san!* Papa-*san!*"

Across the hall the daughter calls loudly. It is time for bed. Mamasan is upstairs in bed. The kitchen light is off; so is the dining room. The clock is a tattler. The time of man is just beginning; the theme a helplessness; action the seeds of tomorrow.

I want to talk to someone. I want to talk and listen and answer. I want to sing in a chorus in tune with the rest of the crowd. I too want to join and laugh and joke. I want sometimes to tell all the people what I know and how little I know.

I cannot flee the people's world. I am more like an inarticulate person than anyone else; the indignation for want of expression to be ignited in some little source: insignificant, impotent, a dud.

Did you note one day the sun was thus and later returned to gaze again and it was thus, but you know all was changed, the sun, the earth, yourself, the nations, the oceans.

One minute you were always light-hearted and wise-cracking. You had the sense of hearing and your friends acknowledging it. You laughed your way out of difficulties, making a lark of life. You heard laughter and you laughed. Friends came around and slapped your back. Words came easy. Gestures came abruptly in childish natural movements. And in turn of a minute you had dignity you never knew you possessed. You never lost your sense of hearing, but a day of a joke on your wife and family and friends turned the spring.

You were you yesterday. You are you today. You sit in a hole you made yourself. You sit and grin privately. You put one over. It is fun to separate for awhile from your family and friends, and descend or ascend in a different role. It's all right if you are a movie actor, dropping one role and taking up another. Unless you're an actor such a holiday is difficult on earth. You must drop one role or the other. This is the saddest thing on earth because we are all actors in our poor-lit stages, unsung, unheralded, pitied for the sake of our characters and not for our roles. One minute we are a dreamer, another minute a comic, another time a banker, a poet, a statesman, a gambler, a philanthropist, a drunk, a reverend, a murderer. All this is possible to attain in a single day. We turn and twist at a moment's mood, and the force of our surroundings is mirrored in the roles.

Did you ever have a time when you'd sit in a dark room and know every man in the world? Did you remember the time you'd have such a feeling? Was it when you were happy in a revelry or when you were alone and realized your friends had stayed away very long and you did not go out and seek them?

I sat in the kitchen and watched the women come and go. I sat in the living room among my men friends and watched them. There's really nothing to report and everything to understand. Often friendship is a fog and often you will know total strangers more intimately. I found this out in the park where I go almost daily. A warm afternoon in the park among total strangers is a lift. You talk and you are free.

I sat among my people in the living room without talk; and as I sat there without laughter, just smiling, I knew they were assembled there without laughter. I remember the way they sat around and talked. I knew they were laughing at times and were without real laughter and were feverishly together for a real one.

It was on a sunny morning three hours before noon when I had walked for seven blocks and had come to a park. It was a park I had never seen before. It was the beginning of a fresh idea and the resurrection of myself; the park life of this particular park and the parks of other American cities and Berlin, London, Tokyo, Moscow, Paris, Rome were no different; and the park life and the living room life and the dark room life were all the same dough; and laughter or no laughter was the same; and death or deathless was alike; and a joke or a tragedy was out of the same stem; and the man the same.

I sat and talked with a man who came from the Oklahoma fields. I saw him but once. He never mentioned that he was of the dust bowl clan once but it was printed all over him. A man who came from Indiana talked one day for hours. He said he once worked in a nursery where he hauled the soil in a wheelbarrow. A grocer sat beside me and talked of the business conditions. A young idealist rabidly sought me for a follower. One day there was a retired capitalist sitting and talking a few seats from me, and he looked the same as anyone else. I completely lost time that day and overlooked lunch and was late cooking supper. My wife gave me hell.

Turn the disk of the earth: a bed is soaring. The clouds roar. The rivers dry. The skies drop. The sun melts. The man is bigger than the earth. Why? A dream is a better production than Warner Brothers pictures. A dream is the reality in hope; and reality the nightmare of a dream reversed. Destruction and education hand in hand. Red Cross and butchery on the same fields. Death and birth in Ward E. Asylum and earth together: fences. Barefoot and shoes, and nudism and morality. One man and one woman. One man and two women. One woman and two men. One man and many women. One woman and many men. The impatience of man. The patience of man. He sleeps. He wakes. The sleep of a man and the disk of earth continues.

Through the cracks of a cream shade the light pours in the room. The birds sing and the milk trucks rumble by. The sun is up and the room is cold. Jetliners fly; the trains whistle; the shouts of the neighbors recall the earth; the consciousness of mind awakens the presence of being.

It is morning and man is no different; the philosophy of man no different; his responsibilities are no different, his roles unchanged, and his fantasies descending. The man in bed blinks his eyes, and the rivers roll, gas and electric is on, the clock ticks, the clothes are pressed, the shoes need mending, the breakfast to make for four, the furniture to be dusted, and a park stroll scheduled.

Darkness is over, the black is grey, prison grey, and a brighter hue is present at last. And a man accepts his affliction: senseless vacuum with the waves of the earth in motion. Motionless, his nerves unflinching he attempts communication. (Wife! Son! Daughter! Wake up . . . new morning!) End of a man of no senses: Now not only deaf but visionless, dumb, feelingless, colorless, numb . . . only a sixth sense serenity. Smile, rejoice: I was once here. Soon not a trace of my presence would remain. But who cares? (I care, says the government. I care, says the church. I do, say the friends.) I second the motion . . . while I am still alive. While I am alive, I shall smile and laugh, and in spirit grab the grits of life, scraping for crumbs while cooking up the great feast of life.

—1935

# 1936

THERE IS SOMETHING in the way I feel toward the year 1936 that I shall be sure to remember. Perhaps it may be that I am living today, that I am alive and am striving toward my hope, that I feel so strongly the tang and the bracing weather of today and the more todays to come. It is the year I shall recall later as the time of change in the conduct of life and outlook. I like to explain away the change and the song of it here but that is a hopeless task just now. I must simply say it is the year of 1936 and was the year and let it go at that. But if I should tell you how I feel today about 1936, I might be able to do something about it.

I began suddenly or slowly, it does not matter, to want, to desire, to sink my teeth into everything I could grasp, to everything I see, hear, smell, taste, etc. I wanted to do everything, I wanted to know women, I wanted to know the white people, the minds of my generation and people, the Nisei, the nature of our parents, the Issei, the culture of Japan, the culture of America, of life as a whole. I wanted to go from the country to the city and from the city to the country. I began to move, I began by joining the Eden Japanese American Citizens League, I went to the girls' homes, I went to see the boys, listened to the lecture of Dr. Alfred Adler, the psychoanalyst, listened to Kagawa in English at the Oakland Auditorium, and also in Japanese at Wanto Gakuen. I listened to the Japanese girl talking about her beautiful girl friend, Tsuyuko, who is wealthy and unhappy; the Tsuyuko I could not forget. I heard her speak of another girl who had been raised and educated in Japan, called over by the parents to join

25

them in California. I heard of the girl who had ruined her chance for
marriage and livelihood in America by her temperament and objec-
tions, and was now returning to Japan on the next boat. I heard my
friend speak of her friend as strong-willed who finally broke down and
wept before the sailing day. She was afraid of her friend's rash nature
and of her decision to return to Japan and the consequent fate. As I
listened to the girl, of her life, gossip, experiences, talks, rumors, I
saw how much I did not know of life, the limitations of my life, and
how much more she was close to the life of the people and of herself.
This girl (I have been grateful to her ever since) drove me restless with
her knowledge and her life, to seek, to experience something of my own.

I do not know when I began or perhaps, I do not know when I began
to notice, to really notice the lives and the people inhabitating today
in the year of 1936. I do not know exactly who or what event was
the first experience; the lives and the people of 1936 are so assembled
together, alike in usefulness, that I cannot place one individual or the
individuals above another but must recall them together, hand in hand.

From the morning I began visiting the Japanese dentist in the heart
of downtown district, to have my teeth fixed, the every day, the days
that come around simply and plainly every day, became my interest
and love. I thought it lovely that each day became an adventure; I
thought it lovely enough when I realized that every day, plain and
simple, was unlike any other day. One day I would meet the white
elevator girl who would take me up to the dentist's floor and she would
say something about the weather, or about the dentist visiting, or
about the tasty smell coming into the elevator shaft from the candy
kitchen in the basement, and then I would not meet her for days.

On another day I might be riding home on the bus and would sit
alongside a middle-aged man and a college student as I have precisely
done. I would find out as I watched the middle-aged man striking
up a conversation with the college student, that he was a writer, a
writer of cowboy stories, who had sold a half-dozen stories or so to the
magazines. And I would listen to his theories and his battles with
writing in the evenings and listening, I would begin to think about his
office (presumably an office man) and his family. I did not meet the
same college student again but listening to that one conversation just
before noonday, I found out he was once interested in writing but
now had quit. He was a quiet youth, gentlemanly and of generous
nature. The day and the meeting, and the impression would end just
that way and I knew it was the end of another day. And with the
weather of the days I found it the same. One day it would be warm,
another day too hot for comfort, some days cloudy, another time
windy, cold or raining, foggy, drizzling. To go further, it is true that a

single day is a variation of temperature, light, etc., and I thought this was a lovely way of prolonging interest in life, to desire something that is yet to be and is not so sure about becoming that way, that uncertain as our lives may be we have come more to love the days that are ours.

While I was crazily pursuing everything, everything in life, wanting to know, wanting to experience, wanting to see the spark and the lives of men, wanting to see the spark of life and the spark of individuals, I could have been a poet. I could have claimed the stars and the universe, the earth, the soil, the birds, and the gentlefolks. Today I am not the same; I am still pursuing, still crazily lusting, but I do not and cannot claim the stars and the universe, the earth and the like, or even more so claim the women, the nations, the wealth, the patents, and the life. I cannot claim, when I come to think of it, even the petty things and I cannot claim the tools, I cannot claim the materials and the art of life. This is so I cannot claim the year of 1936 though I am in love with it, though I am glad I am living today. I simply sit here in my den, in the presence of the year 1936, present with its shortness, death, and variation, and also, conscious of the rarity, 1936, the only year to be 1936. This leads me to the ending, to the finish of this piece and the commencement of the brother years 1937, 1938, 1939, 1940, and so on, wanting to know, everything, restless, hungering, seeking, crazily . . . .

It is just as well to end anything like this on Monday of his life as well as on Saturday. It is the same, the ending and the beginning, and I shall take one day, Monday, the representative of all the Mondays, and the representative of Tuesdays, Wednesdays, Thursdays, Fridays, Saturdays, Sundays, and of the year 1936, as the spokesman, the chronicle, the record, and as perhaps, a farce.

I will begin easily for myself, thinking from the time I rise for the flower market to work, thinking as I go along, remembering, tasting, visioning the faces I've seen and the events that were to be Monday. I will go to the market to sell flowers from 7 A.M. to 8:30 A.M. and finishing that I am through at the market, free to go home and turn over the soil, water the plants, cut the flowers, etc. On Mondays I cannot go home early; it is the day of adventures, because I am going to the dentist, and because there are many hours to fill between the market work and the dentist's appointment. The first thing I do when I am free for the morning (I notice) is to go to the public library on Fourteenth and Grove. It is fascinating to see people reading, and it is fascinating to realize that here one can become learned and be up-to-date as anywhere else. But meeting the man, the incident that happened today on Monday that makes Mondays memorable, did not

happen upstairs or downstairs in the reading room nor in the fiction
room, the non-fiction room, but down the hall on the first floor in the
men's rest room. I do not remember precisely the beginning of our
chat with this man, the custodian of the library halls. He was leaning
against the wall puffing his cigarette rapidly, taking time out for a
smoke when I entered the place and our conversation began. He was
my size, a small man, quite bald, a man you would not believe had
gone a foot out of California or Oakland even. He began talking, and
the minute he opened his mouth I knew he was anxious to have someone to talk to. He began talking of his days at sea and I was surprised
at the news, surprised that the custodian of a public library could
ever think of such an adventure of life.

"I have been on the sea for twenty years," he said. "I have been to
many ports of the world, Bombay, Liverpool, Marseilles, Yokohama,
everywhere, coming in, going out, around the world. For twenty
years I saw very little but the sea."

"Twenty years is a long time," I said. "You must love the sea very
much."

"I did not love the sea," he said. "I was much more afraid to starve
on land. I was afraid I could get no job of any kind, I was afraid of
knowing nothing, and I was afraid of starving."

I shall not make up anything of the meeting; I will leave it alone. It
happened as I told you and it ended briefly without the usual rounds
of drinks. In fact there is nothing unusual to this meeting and there is
nothing unusual about his twenty years on the sea; only the fact that
we talked and were simply alive and warm, to talk, and to listen,
wanting to know, wanting to give, that the incident became memorable, that I should be able to remember it today.

I was ten minutes late for the appointment and the Japanese dentist
was waiting for me. I have been going to this dentist for almost a year
and every time I step from the waiting room to the laboratory, I am
reminded, not of teeth-fixing, but something of the experience and the
sensitiveness of this artist of molars. He is, what Sherwood Anderson
would call, an old craftsman. I have listened to the philosophies of the
philosophy, from the books to the philosophers, the scholars, priests,
and the masters of the past and they are all right; I do not junk them.
But coming here in the laboratory, in the presence of this small Japanese, I forget many things, I forget philosophies, the books. It is an experience like a moth flying toward the red-hot lamp; myself leaping
kangaroo-like to shake hands and derive some good and warmth from
this man, an alive one. With this in mind I forget my teeth and the
dentist begins to possess my teeth, till the teeth, my teeth, belong back

and forth, from one to the other, belonging to the wanting-to-know, belonging to the wanting-to-give, till the teeth of the world (becoming the materials) becomes one taken possession of, taken care of, becoming relative one and all.

This is not what we talk of, the dentist and I, but if we were able to grease our tongues smoother and nobler, I think, since we are men, and alive today, it would be how we feel about the teeth, about love, about work, about hope, about life.

Every time I visit my brother's shop in Oakland I remember the unidentified day when I had a haircut at Tony's in the presence of two customers. This was out in the suburbs. There are times when I see Tony out on the sidewalk walking back and forth, wearing the barber's apron, smoking a cigar. He would wave his hand when he saw me. Sometimes when I went slow he would shout, "Hello, boy! Where are you going?"

"Hello, Tony," I said, "Oakland."

He would wave his hand again and smile. The day I am particular about was such a day as this. I went in for a haircut. Before I was there five minutes two customers came in a minute apart. I remember this meeting at the barber shop because Tony and his two latest customers, and myself were present and responsible for the effect. It is why I also remember that the event has something in common with my brother in his new rooms above his shop. The four of us at the barber shop did not talk about anything important, I remember. The Spaniard was kidding Tony about the warmth of the shop. (This was in December and Tony had a tiny coal oil stove burning for heat.) All the while the two, the Spaniard and the Italian, kidded back and forth. In the corner a big Mexican was smiling and I, Japanese, sat in the chair smiling. I could not make up the nationalities present there that afternoon at the barber shop. The moment I caught on to the bizarreness of the meeting, the novelty of four nationalities assembled in one tiny shop, I began to think of America. This was not a new thing to the old stock of America but to me as a Japanese American, it was something. If one tiny barber shop could have four nationalities at one time, how many does America house? Then, I could believe the vastness and the goodness of America's project; this is the place, the earth where the brothers and the races meet, mingle and share, and the most likely place, the most probable part of the earth to seek peace and goodwill through relations with the rest of the world. It is for this reaction I think of my brother, living in his new surroundings, in the city, among the peoples of the earth, rooming in the same house with half-a-dozen nationalities, among them a Russian doctor, his best friend. I think of his life ahead in the city of America, I think of the thousands of untouched relations between the nationalities, the colors, the creeds, and the hour, the time and his opportunity of being.

I met Sheldon Brown's father in the morning of a Monday in 1936 and I shall end my day, my 1936, with the remembrance of Sheldon's dad because it is fitting, and for the reason that the meeting took place in the morning of my 1936 which is the afternoon, the evening of my piece and also the morning again. I had known Sheldon and his brother Bob since grammar school days in Oakland. That was fifteen years ago; it does not concern here, today. I want to say something of Sheldon's father who came to see me, a friendly visit, and we began talking about his sons, my friends. And the father of these two boys, now grown, twenty-seven and twenty-four respectively, laughed and chuckled as he related the uncertain and certain, an interesting career of the younger son. Bob, he related, believed he had found the medium, the business of his life, in acting, to be an actor. "After three years of college," the father chuckled and was amused at his son's notions, "he wants to be an actor. He is today, studying dramatics, earning his bread as an art model in San Francisco."

"That is fine," I said to the father. He laughed heartily and one could see he had taken fancy to Bob's ambition. The family, he said, would not interfere. It is no use; Bob tried his hand at carpentry, (his father's trade), and was indifferent in interest and work. The father was skeptical of Bob's life, career, and the last I saw of him (the father), in 1936, with his amused, chuckling face, he was fancying and thrilling at the new generation with their struggles, soberliness, loneliness, that is, of 1936.

All this will be forgotten, about Sheldon's father and how Bob rose or fell, how at one time such and such a thing happened and that there ever was a year called 1936, and that there ever was a writer for its days, and that the people of 1936 were once living. All this will be forgotten; this is logical, this is not important. But what I am trying to get at, to put over to you, is that in 1936 once there was a youth wanting to know, wanting to know so badly he wanted to stab at everything, everything in life. He was living once, the youth of 1936, and is living again in 1937, 1938, and so on, till the time of man is no more. I am not weeping for him; I am glad for him, I cannot weep and feel sorry for something that is living and will be living long after our death.

—1936

# Abalone, Abalone, Abalone

BEFORE MR. ABE went away I used to see him quite often at his nursery. He was a carnation grower just as I am one today. At noontime I used to go to his front porch and look at his collection of abalone shells.

They were lined up side by side against the side of his house on the front porch. I was curious as to why he bothered to collect them. It was lot of bother polishing them. I had often seen him sit for hours on Sundays and noon hours polishing each one of the shells with the greatest of care. Of course I knew these abalone shells were pretty. When the sun strikes the insides of these shells it is something beautiful to behold. But I could not understand why he continued collecting them when the front porch was practically full.

He used to watch for me every noon hour. When I appeared he would look out of his room and bellow, "Hello, young man!"

"Hello, Abe-*san*," I said. "I came to see the abalone shells."

Then he came out of the house and we sat on the front porch. But he did not tell me why he collected these shells. I think I have asked him dozens of times but each time he closed his mouth and refused to answer.

"Are you going to pass this collection of abalone shells on to your children?" I said.

"No," he said. "I want my children to collect for themselves. I wouldn't give it to them."

"Why?" I said. "When you die?"

Mr. Abe shook his head. "No. Not even when I die," he said. "I couldn't give the children what I see in these shells. The children must go out for themselves and find their own shells."

31

"Why, I thought this collecting hobby of abalone shells was a simple affair," I said.

"It is simple. Very simple," he said. But he would not tell me further.

For several years I went steadily to his front porch and looked at the beautiful shells. His collection was getting larger and larger. Mr. Abe sat and talked to me and on each occasion his hands were busy polishing the shells.

"So you are still curious?" he said.

"Yes," I said.

One day while I was hauling the old soil from the benches and replacing it with new soil I found an abalone shell half buried in the dust between the benches. So I stopped working. I dropped my wheelbarrow and went to the faucet and washed the abalone shell with soap and water. I had a hard time taking the grime off the surface.

After forty minutes of cleaning and polishing the old shell it became interesting. I began polishing both the outside and the inside of the shell. I found after many minutes of polishing I could not do very much with the exterior side. It had scabs of the sea which would not come off by scrubbing and the surface itself was rough and hard. And in the crevices the grime stuck so that even with a needle it did not become clean.

But on the other side, the inside of the shell, the more I polished the more lustre I found. It had me going. There were colors which I had not seen in the abalone shells before or anywhere else. The different hues, running beserk in all directions, coming together in harmony. I guess I could say they were not unlike a rainbow which men once symbolized. As soon as I thought of this I thought of Mr. Abe.

I remember running to his place, looking for him. "Abe-*san*!" I said when I found him. "I know why you are collecting the abalone shells!"

He was watering the carnation plants in the greenhouse. He stopped watering and came over to where I stood. He looked me over closely for awhile and then his face beamed.

"All right," he said. "Do not say anything. Nothing, mind you. When you have found the reason why you must collect and preserve them, you do not have to say anything more."

"I want you to see it, Abe-*san*," I said.

"All right. Tonight," he said. "Where did you find it?"

"In my old greenhouse, half buried in the dust," I said.

He chuckled. "That is pretty far from the ocean," he said, "but pretty close to you."

At each noon hour I carried my abalone shell and went over to

Mr. Abe's front porch. While I waited for his appearance I kept my-self busy polishing the inside of the shell with a rag.

One day I said, "Abe-*san*, now I have three shells."

"Good!" he said. "Keep it up!"

"I have to keep them all," I said. "They are very much alike and very much different."

"Well! Well!" he said and smiled.

That was the last I saw of Abe-*san*. Before the month was over he sold his nursery and went back to Japan. He brought his collection along and thereafter I had no one to talk to at the noon hour. This was before I discovered the fourth abalone shell, and I should like to see Abe-*san* someday and watch his eyes roll as he studies me whose face is now akin to the collectors of shells or otherwise.

—1937

# The Distant Call
# of the Deer

PERHAPS YOU'VE HEARD him on one of the amateur hours around the Bay Region. If you have you will know him and all you have to do is follow what I have to say and perhaps you may add something more to the tale. If you do not know him already I must tell you. Sooner or later you will be hearing stories about him and I would like first to acquaint him to you.

Togo Satoshima is not my friend but I know him. He lives in the tankhouse back of the house which he owns. In the house he lives with his wife and five children; he eats, sleeps, and talks in the house but when he goes up to the tankhouse sometimes he forgets to come back to the house. He has a cot up there and whenever he is tired he lies down for a nap.

When Togo Satoshima is up in the tankhouse the neighbors generally know it. You couldn't be private with a pipe like his and his talent. The Japanese call the instrument *shakuhachi*. It is a flute-like piece of a bamboo with a number of holes which your fingers fool with. And when Togo Satoshima goes up to the tankhouse and picks up the *shakuhachi* there is no one who can call him down. His wife gave up long ago. Recently the neighbors called a meeting to plan how they could persuade Togo Satoshima to quit his call of art. The neighbors are still wondering whether it is easier on them to muffle all the dog howls in the neighborhood when Togo begins blowing or to allow the dog and cat howls to have voice and maybe drown out the music. Meanwhile some of the folks have gone so far as to bring down from the attic the old radio earphones to protect themselves when Togo Satoshima really gets going.

No matter how many ways Togo Satoshima plays the music you will get to know he is playing "The Distant Call of the Deer." It is the only piece he knows.

Togo Satoshima has an old phonograph up in the tankhouse which you must crank to play the records. On each practice session you can hear in the beginning some master of Japan blowing a *shakuhachi*. That is the record playing "The Distant Call of the Deer." After several rounds of listening, Togo Satoshima accompanies him for more rounds. And when he is really warmed up Togo Satoshima begins his solos.

Soon he began to have the undivided attention of the neighborhood. People who did not trouble to know him before began to notice him.

"What is Satoshima-*san* up to?" someone would ask.

"He is crazy," another would answer. "Something in his head got mixed up. He is crazy."

"He's too old to go overboard like this," the third one would say. "But does he know it?"

Togo Satoshima isn't any too young to go gallivanting around and do crazy things. He is fifty-three this year and has a twenty-five-year-old daughter to think of. Togo's wife keeps nagging him about their girl. "She must have a husband real soon," she says to him. But Togo Satoshima is above petty matters. You do not know Togo until he gets inside his tankhouse.

The funny part of Togo Satoshima's drive for art is his utter lack of ambition to become professional. Perhaps he is not that far gone. But when he began to cavort around with the young people, vying for honors and prizes at the amateur hours and nights, his wife threw up her hands and went into tantrums. The neighbors stood around speechless.

It began one day when Togo Satoshima came to realize there were amateur hours and nights and there were other amateurs in this world besides himself. When he learned how big his world really was, he came into his own. That was his opinion. He became more daring and began to look about in the new big world of his.

One of his youthful friends tipped him off about radio auditions and trials on the amateur nights. When he found this new goal to work for he went more often into the tankhouse. Sometimes even in the daytime the neighbors began to hear the notes of "The Distant Call of the Deer."

There is no question that Togo Satoshima is an amazing person. I do not know how many times he did not qualify for the amateur hours. He must have had dozens of auditions with the different amateur hour programs besides the auditions for the amateur nights. Anyway he finally got into one of the amateur hours later which did not ₄et him anything but a few votes.

However when the few votes came his way Togo Satoshima firmly believed in himself and his call of art. There was no stopping him then. After that he tried many times to qualify for the amateur hours and nights without success. When he could not get in for a long stretch of time he went out to parties and benefits and played his *shakuhachi*. And each time he played it was "The Distant Call of the Deer."

Meanwhile Togo Satoshima's neighborhood returned to normal. The playing of *shakuhachi* in the tankhouse was less heard. The neighbors began to sleep early and were undisturbed, and the dogs of the block had time to recuperate from throat troubles. His wife and children saw Togo Satoshima often in the house. Everything was back to normal but it did not last long.

I suppose the whole thing happened because Togo Satoshima was really trying all the time. When he was quiet he was not all through but was getting ready for the debut. His chance really did come weeks later when he was billed among the fourteen contestants to try for the three prizes donated by the Tsurui Jewelry Co. This particular amateur night, which was the most important event of Togo Satoshima's life, thus far, was sponsored by Asahi Athletic Club.

Out of the fourteen contestants who performed that night in the Asahi Auditorium all but Togo Satoshima were youngsters. Youngsters who were in high schools or the graduates who worked somewhere or did not have jobs. There were three contestants of grade-school ages but this did not stop Togo Satoshima from doing his best.

When the applause machine finally had done its duty for the evening, contestant number seven which was Togo Satoshima, won third prize. By the hand clapping of the audience we could not tell who was the third prize winner but when the applause machine chose Togo Satoshima for third prize there was no end of clapping by the audience. Perhaps they were clapping for the age of the contestant number seven, not Togo Satoshima. I do not know. Anyway it does not matter now. No one could hold back Togo Satoshima that night. Late into the night he was still passing around cigars, jumping up and down like a kid.

Togo Satoshima is back in the tankhouse again, burning electric till wee hours in the morning, blowing his *shakuhachi*. Over and over the notes of "The Distant Call of the Deer" float and jar into the air and the dog howls join in unison. The neighbors' old earphones appear again. Togo Satoshima's wife holds up her hands again in despair and goes about her work in the house with the daybreak.

And with the news of Togo Satoshima's prize-winning feat the neighbors are little more worried and the end of the tankhouse episodes is nowhere near.

—1937

# Japanese Hamlet

HE USED TO come to the house and ask me to hear him recite. Each time he handed me a volume of *The Complete Works of William Shakespeare*. He never forgot to do that. He wanted me to sit in front of him, open the book, and follow him as he recited his lines. I did willingly. There was little for me to do in the evenings so when Tom Fukunaga came over I was ready to help out almost any time. And as his love for Shakespeare's plays grew with the years he did not want anything else in the world but to be a Shakespearean actor.

Tom Fukunaga was a schoolboy in a Piedmont home. He had been one since his freshman days in high school. When he was thirty-one he was still a schoolboy. Nobody knew his age but he and the relatives. Every time his relatives came to the city they put up a roar and said he was a good-for-nothing loafer and ought to be ashamed of himself for being a schoolboy at this age.

"I am not loafing," he told his relatives. "I am studying very hard."

One of his uncles came often to the city to see him. He tried a number of times to persuade Tom to quit stage hopes and schoolboy attitude. "Your parents have already disowned you. Come to your senses," he said. "You should go out and earn a man's salary. You are alone now. Pretty soon even your relatives will drop you."

"That's all right," Tom Fukunaga said. He kept shaking his head until his uncle went away.

When Tom Fukunaga came over to the house he used to tell me about his parents and relatives in the country. He told me in particular about the uncle who kept coming back to warn and persuade him.

39

Tom said he really was sorry for Uncle Bill to take the trouble to
see him.

"Why don't you work for someone in the daytime and study at
night?" I said to Tom.

"I cannot be bothered with such a change at this time," he said.
"Besides, I get five dollars a week plus room and board. That is enough
for me. If I should go out and work for someone I would have to pay
for room and board besides carfare so I would not be richer. And even
if I should save a little more it would not help me become a better
Shakespearean actor."

When we came down to the business of recitation there was no
recess. Tom Fukunaga wanted none of it. He would place a cup of
water before him and never touch it. "Tonight we'll begin with
Hamlet," he said many times during the years. Hamlet was his favorite
play. When he talked about Shakespeare to anyone he began by mentioning Hamlet. He played parts in other plays but always he came
back to Hamlet. This was his special role, the role which would estab-
lish him in Shakespearean history.

There were moments when I was afraid that Tom's energy and time
were wasted and I helped along to waste it. We were miles away from
the stage world. Tom Fukunaga had not seen a backstage. He was just
as far from the stagedoor in his thirties as he was in his high school
days. Sometimes as I sat holding Shakespeare's book and listening to
Tom I must have looked worried and discouraged.

"Come on, come on!" he said. "Have you got the blues?"

One day I told him the truth: I was afraid we were not getting anywhere, that perhaps we were attempting the impossible. "If you could
contact the stage people it might help," I said. "Otherwise we are
wasting our lives."

"I don't think so," Tom said. "I am improving every day. That is
what counts. Our time will come later."

That night we took up Macbeth. He went through his parts smoothly. This made him feel good. "Some day I'll be the ranking Shakespearean actor," he said.

Sometimes I told him I liked best to hear him recite the sonnets. I
thought he was better with the sonnets than in the parts of Macbeth
or Hamlet.

"I'd much rather hear you recite his sonnets, Tom." I said.

"Perhaps you like his sonnets best of all," he said. "Hamlet is my
forte. I know I am at my best playing Hamlet."

For a year Tom Fukunaga did not miss a week coming to the house.
Each time he brought a copy of Shakespeare's complete works and

asked me to hear him say the lines. For better or worse he was not a bit downhearted. He still had no contact with the stage people. He did not talk about his uncle who kept coming back urging him to quit. I found out later that his uncle did not come to see him any more.

In the meantime Tom stayed at the Piedmont home as a schoolboy. He accepted his five dollars a week just as he had done years ago when he was a freshman at Piedmont High. This fact did not bother Tom at all when I mentioned it to him. "What are you worrying for?" he said. "I know I am taking chances. I went into this with my eyes open so don't worry."

But I could not get over worrying about Tom Fukunaga's chances. Every time he came over I felt bad for he was wasting his life and for the fact that I was mixed in it. Several times I told him to go somewhere and find a job. He laughed. He kept coming to the house and asked me to sit and hear him recite Hamlet.

The longer I came to know Tom the more I wished to see him well off in business or with a job. I got so I could not stand his coming to the house and asking me to sit while he recited. I began to dread his presence in the house as if his figure reminded me of my part in the mock play that his life was, and the prominence that my house and attention played.

One night I became desperate. "That book is destroying you, Tom. Why don't you give this up for awhile?"

He looked at me curiously without a word. He recited several pages and left early that evening.

Tom did not come to the house again. I guess it got so that Tom could not stand me any more than his uncle and parents. When he quit coming I felt bad. I knew he would never abandon his ambition. I was equally sure that Tom would never rank with the great Shakespearean actors, but I could not forget his simple persistence.

One day, years later, I saw him on the Piedmont car at Fourteenth and Broadway. He was sitting with his head buried in a book and I was sure it was a copy of Shakespeare's. For a moment he looked up and stared at me as if I were a stranger. Then his face broke into a smile and he raised his hand. I waved back eagerly.

"How are you, Tom?" I shouted.

He waved his hand politely again but did not get off, and the car started up Broadway.

—1939

# II
# THE DAILY WORK

# Confessions of an
# Unknown Writer

"Go and buy a coat and a hat," I told her. "You're going to a wedding and your coat is five years old and that hat is old style." My mother was going to a wedding in the city and yesterday she wished she had something new to wear to the affair. I was in her room with a batch of old magazines I had bought in the city. Nickel apiece for *Story*, *Harper*, *New Yorker*, *Atlantic Monthly*, *Fiction Parade*, *Scribner's*, and *Writer's Digest*. I wanted her to go in new clothes so she would feel good, so she would feel she belonged to the age, the year, the feminine fashion of the day. I wanted her to feel good when she joined her friends at the party.

"Everything's a bargain now," I said. "Twenty dollars will do. Buy it tomorrow."

"No," she said. "I don't want it. It isn't your wedding. My clothes will do."

"Oh, go ahead and buy it," I said.

"I don't want it," she said. "I don't want a new coat. Just get your story in some magazine and I'll feel better."

I sat on the bed and leafed *The Atlantic*. I wanted very much to appear in a magazine and hadn't got in. I had grown old and was a half-writer and a half-nurseryman. This was no place to feel bad but after having six stories returned from the magazines that afternoon I felt rotten. I wanted to talk of the future but I couldn't. Sometimes if you're a writer it's fun to talk of the future. It's very nice to see

45

something that'll be you in the future if the luck's with you. But something's been wrong with me lately: I was a dead-beat. I didn't want her to know how I was feeling but she knew how I was feeling these days, and it made it all the worse.

I sat there in her room holding the magazines and thinking of names and dates. Dreiser wrote his *Sister Carrie* at twenty-eight; Thomas Wolfe began at twenty-eight; Dostoyevsky at twenty-five; Saroyan at twenty-four; Hemingway in the early twenties. It wasn't just the desperation from lack of time. It wasn't just the literary side of the matter. It was everything. It was time I was thinking of myself as a solitary man in the world: the man alone like everyone else, matured and immatured. The man alone as a writer, and the man alone as a means of living. I couldn't be a writer and I was one.

When you are young everything is simple outside of yourself. When you get a little older you begin to see everything is not simple including yourself. And when you are about to die and about to be death itself, everything becomes simple again. We know the cycle of life. We have scientifically searched the individual cases over and over so today we know how the human beings act and react, and why. We know the law and order. We paint things up these days but we know it's the old stuff. The meaning of work today is same as the meaning of work before Christ. To get to the point: one writer writes and another writer follows and writes. When you think of it seriously it's curious. After the millions of writers through the ages get through with expression what has the latest writer got that wasn't expressed before unless it's after-death mystery? A tailor tailors and another tailor follows suit and tailors. It's simple: practical use. A scientist experiments and another scientist adds, and that's understandable: progress. You might say a writer follows the millions of writers for moral, spiritual, and material progress and let it go at that. That's a generous tag and sometimes it turns out comical. You might say writers bob up every minute or so because of the imperfect world. And you might add that there will always be writers on earth because you know man's world will never be perfect. I won't argue with anybody about this opinion because I am a little older and know everything is not so simple, including myself the writer.

If you are a Japanese or have Japanese friends who talk you will understand the situation a young man is in when the friendly men and women of the older generation come around to you and talk about marriage. They begin mentioning names of the girls and describing their personalities. This probably won't happen to the boys who go out early and pick a girl and marry her. It won't happen to the veterans of love affairs because they are left alone, and justly so on account of their abilities. It will happen to men who are shy and respectable and to men who are still unattached at a respectable age and have had no luck. Well, this particular friend comes in every once in a while and starts rattling off the girls' names to me.

"Why don't you marry?" he keeps asking me. There are several others but I won't mention them.

"I don't want to marry just now," I tell this friend of mine.

"Why?" he comes right back, and I must tell him the truth to make him go away and shut up.

"I want to write," I tell him. This is an unreasonable and inadequate answer but it was all I could get out of myself.

"You can marry and write at the same time," my particular friend says. "They mix well. Why wait for a better spring?"

I couldn't answer this one because I haven't had experience in that line. Anyhow I shook my head vigorously and said, "I want to write." I didn't say it lamely. I was very sure of myself, and I don't know why. I stood him off very well. "Yes," I admitted, "you can marry and write. You can marry if you have money to set up a home."

But what struggling writer has time enough to write and have money enough to set up a new home for a bride? You either write and get in a little money and marry or you marry and become acclimated with everything, including money, and then write. It's an angle, one way or the other. You have no money and you have no girl or you have no money and you have a girl. But in either case you are to write, and also live.

Sometimes I kick myself inwardly for being a fool. My friends who came out of the school in the same year or later have become substantial citizens in their community. George Matsuo has a good-sized bank account and is single. What has a guy like that got to worry about unless he has crazy ideas? Tadashi Nozato is a good salaried salesman plus bonus and commission. Averages two hundred a month or more, owns a home, and has a beautiful wife. Tommy Doi is a hustling grocer. Has a wife and three kids, three smooth-running stores, and owns a Buick. Shigeo Kawashima now a big-shot in an important company. Good old Tack Toyama, now Doctor Toyama, physician-surgeon. I could go on for pages but I must eventually return to myself.

In the middle of drilling a hole in my abscessed tooth I confided to my dentist that I was secretly writing. He wasn't a bit surprised when I confessed. He is an artist of dentistry because he makes you forget he is fixing your teeth, and when you hear him talking you are admitting to yourself that a dentist has been working all the time. His fingers are sensitive to the touch. They detect the feel of a nerve center when a drill is working so you can enjoy a conversation with him. We were talking about the structure and the resistance and the decay of not only the teeth but life itself. He looked at me, when I said I was writing, as if I were a young tooth or a young cypress. He didn't know what sort of writing I was doing but his smile of "Ah, good for you," made me forget bad writing and the blue days. "Take fifty years," he told me. "Take a lifetime." He had married late and accomplishments came late. When he was young he had a hell of a time. "I once had to go around to the white dentists and solicit for dental plate work," he said. "I had opened an office on Twelfth and Broadway and no customers came for months. The plate work paid the rent and a sign on my door and I was fortunate to eat." First it was the problem of an abscessed tooth; then it was the resistance and decay of life; and now it was writing we talk about.

I am sitting in my mother's room thinking of the roll of my short life. If I were to die tonight I would leave nothing behind. With death I would be forever erased; with life I would be forever divorced. If I were to find myself alive tomorrow morning at eight I would still be a half-writer and a half-nurseryman. I would put every ounce of my body behind my words, thinking of death. Tomorrow I would be death seeking life. This is the comical history of my thoughts. This is endless because I am alive. This is comical because I am dead serious. And I would add that my history is like a thousand nights and days: the dots and dashes of a brief light in a smoky city.

"Don't you want to go to the wedding?" I asked mother. It was a foolish question. She was inside the closet taking down her garments and looking them over.

"Yes, I'm going," she said. Then I heard clearly "The Wedding March" on a church organ. I visioned the scene of a toast and dreamed the passing of wedding night. Not far off I heard the drums and bugle calls; the armies marching; and the diplomats rejoicing, sweating, and crying. What do I want to say to the world? Over in the next house a woman has a cancer on the breast and has eleven days to go. A florist is picking his nose for want of business. My barber who has been through the mill spits on love (love in marriage) for the benefit of men customers. Guy Lombardo's sweet lingering music coming out of the men's shack which was once a henhouse. What do I want out of life and what do I want to say? The pussywillows bend with the wind; the magazines go to press without a genius; a writer crosses the ocean in search of material for a book. The letter writer using mannerism. A postcard is for the world to see, and it costs only a cent and a half. Ah, what shall I say? The magnificence of a traffic roar and the grandeur of a stinking city. The lovely silence of death and the lovely silence of life: irresistible, and irritable.

Do you know what capabilities man has? Sit down some day and leisurely think it over. It is a fine story. I am sitting here quietly and I know I have many capabilities. I speak of it because I am sure of myself and know I am not bragging. It is a time like this (sure of myself and know I am not bragging) when I like to sit before a clean white sheet and put my story down. It is this: sometimes I am capable of murder; sometimes I can love; or I am a fanatic or the suppressed or a dreamer or the listless or a coward or any other traits of a being. It is this capability of man which is so natural to occur that I am taking myself as the story and firmly believe its worth. I believe in this capability of man; thus, a saint is no different from a dissipator; a prophet no wiser than a disbeliever; a capitalist and a laborer are pals; a diplomat and a soldier are brothers; a Marian Anderson and an inarticulate are singing the same tune; a producer and a consumer are the union; a citizen and an alien make the flag of man, and; thus, an unpublished and an immortal are writers from the same heart. I believe in man and also disbelieve, and there is no harm. It is temporary as all are fleeting and of decay; and there is no end to it in the ages to come. It is necessary that I should add one climax to this little world of mine: the approach of man to the world (and to himself which is the seed) which makes or breaks the tip of his arrow.

I am back in my little room writing the end of this piece and thinking about myself, the writer. I am settled back and comfortable. I do not need to hurry. My head is clearer and I am returning consciously to the glare of a clean white paper before me. I become smaller and the size of the blank white sheet grows bigger. I become panicky and then dull. The silence of my room which is usually very dear to me begins to irritate me. All I have is myself, I think, and to commune with a clean sheet of paper is the costliest time of my life. I have no place to go, and I have nobody waiting for me. I am a fool, I am a big fool, I think to myself. I am wasting my life on nothing and, like a fool, will continue wasting it forever.

For something to do I rush up to the mirror and look at my face. The biggest little sap, the biggest little sap, I keep saying to myself. What have I done in the past, and what shall be my future? I look at my old face and become sad. I think of my mother and her patience, and her belief in me. This is terrible. This is tragedy. I put the mirror down and look at the familiar objects. My old desk with scattered papers, the old magazines, second-hand books, an old typewriter, and the bare yellow walls. I walk up and down the little room until I become exhausted. Dimly I hear the train whistle, and the trains roar by. It is three in the morning, I think to myself. I sit down in the only seat I have in the room before my typewriter. Then, as I sit for minutes or perhaps hours, it becomes natural for me to sit before the typewriter and face the challenge of a white paper and life. Only then, I realize, I will sit and write even if I should become a fool. I will go on writing for life no matter that may happen for a few mad hours or days, that being a fool will not stop one from becoming what nature had intended him to be.

—1936

# Operator, Operator!

HE DID NOT trouble himself to shave now. He sat by the front window of his room and absently gazed down the street, recognizing nothing but the blurred movements of the traffic in the late afternoon.

The day was not unlike any other days of the past three months. Perhaps he did go out in earnest to look for work in those earlier months. He used to go out every day and look for something. Those were the days when jobs came to him though briefly. But now he need not shave. Nobody wanted to employ him when they saw him in person.

"Yes, we need a gardener," the would-be employer too often told him. "But you're too old. I can't hire you. I'm sorry."

Gunsuke Iwamura heard that many times. He heard that so often he gave up trying to contact new places. He sought the old employers who had at one time or another employed him during the five years he had been in the city. When the old employers saw him they shook their heads and said there were no jobs around. About a month ago he finally gave up the search for work.

Up in his room he sat all day looking out of the window without a trace of emotion. The only time he went out of the boarding house was when he went out to eat. For exercise he paced the floor of his small room until he was tired. Then he climbed into his bed and tried to sleep. But sleep rarely came. In the morning he picked up his purse and counted the coins. At noon just before going out for coffee and doughnuts he counted again and still had two dollars and eleven cents.

51

When he came back to the room the dime for coffee and doughnuts reminded him of his financial status. He tried not to remember the friends who had loaned him money during the years. He had long ago given up adding the total of his debts. To Togami, Saito, Miyazaki, Honda he owned hundreds of dollars. To the rest he owed small amounts but Gunsuke Iwamura now knew he would never be able to repay them.

He had plenty of time to think of the past and himself. He was of the age when people liked to sit back and recall the old times. But Gunsuke Iwamura wanted none of it. He was seventy but had to think of the present.

But each day as he sat by the window looking down the street something of a past would possess him. He thought of his friends who had married and begot families. That was twenty to thirty years ago; that was when he had laughed and told them they were fools. They were comfortable now and their children were doing their bit with the household expenses. And what was he doing all the time? Where was he? The memory took him back to the days on the chicken ranch in Castro Valley; it reminded him of the prune ranches in San Jose where he picked fruits in scorching summers. He thought of the golden days in the twenties when he was in Salinas strawberry fields, earning ten to eleven dollars a day, and every day it was. Now he could not recall where the wages had disappeared. He remembered the day when his back had ached after many seasons of strawberry picking. One day in the midst of a heavy crop he quit. From the Salinas fields he had jumped to the nurseries in Hayward and San Mateo and stayed ten years in the flower industry. Year by year he saw the old men replaced by the younger generation and finally his turn came and was let loose. None of the other nurseries cared to hire old men so he had come to the city.

That was five seasons ago. For five seasons he had been lucky. For five seasons he had been a gardener, part time, or whatever the newspaper ad brought him. For five seasons he was able to live with the assistance of his friends and sporadic jobs. But that was gone—jobs and friends' loans. In fact, everything was gone but two dollars and one cent.

He rose and began to pace about the room. Even the room he had occupied for five years brought uneasiness to him. If Mrs. Yamaguchi, the landlady, weren't tolerant he wouldn't be in the house. He would be out in the street. He owed her four months rent but she let him stay. He thought of his old friends. Good old Togami, Tsudama, Saito, Honda, Miyazaki. He wouldn't forget them. No, if he ever got on his feet again, he'd repay his friends and the landlady. That would be the first thing he'd like to do.

The room was now dark and he reached over and switched the lights on. He sat on the bed and pulled off his shoes. He did not bother to take off his clothes. He lay down and closed his eyes but did not switch the lights off. He thought of the two dollars and one cent . . . all the money he had in the world. If he used it wisely he'd eat for another week. He could eat for another week. What would another week mean to him if things stood as it were? Another week and he'd come face to face with the problems of empty pockets and hungry stomach. Should he do something more than to see another week with his last coins? He visioned the want ad department of the *Herald* and also visioned himself entering the office and filing his entry. He could try a last stab with the want ad notice. He could run his ad for three days. If he should by chance grab hold of a part-time job he could hold on for a spell and there would be hope.

Gunsuke Iwamura fell asleep that night promising himself he'd go to the want ad office the first thing in the morning. For the first time in many weeks he shaved the next morning. It took him several hours to cleanly shave the stubbles off. He went to a restaurant and ate a ten cent meal and set out for the newspaper building.

"I want an ad in the paper," he told the clerk at the desk.

Gunsuke Iwamura wrote: Japanese gardener; part time or day work; capable, experienced, dependable. Grayhill 9187.

After paying the clerk he immediately headed for his room. He had expected to be lifted by the move but his thoughts were filled with dread and uneasiness. Now he realized the strangeness of walking. The streets did queer things. It rose and rose like a hill without a downhill. His feet automatically lifted higher than usual, and sometimes he stumbled unsteadily.

When he was back in the room he felt better. He sat and watched from his window the traffic below which a moment ago terrified him. All day he sat by the window and watched the people hurrying through the streets. He did not go out to eat. With every noise in the hall he leaped up and listened by the door. Was it the phone or Mrs. Yamaguchi coming up to call him? He wouldn't miss the telephone call for anything. If Mrs. Yamaguchi should miss the call it would be his hard luck. He strained himself to hear the phone ring. Afterwards he kept his door open so the phone in the kitchen might be heard.

Gunsuke Iwamura waited all day without a call. He did not go out for lunch. At ten in the evening he gave up and went out and again ate a ten cent meal.

On the second day several phone calls were taken by the landlady but no one called for Gunsuke Iwamura. He did not go out all day, even for meals.

On the third day he sat by the door and tensely listened to the noises in the kitchen. All day he sat rigidly and waited for the call. Nothing happened that day to Gunsuke Iwamura. At eleven that night he looked at his coins and counted sixteen cents. Finally he dropped them in his coat pocket and decided to have breakfast in the morning.

That night Gunsuke Iwamura did not even take off his shoes. He lay on the bed and did not shut off the light. He closed his eyes. He would go again and put an ad in the paper if he had the money. Yes, he would. He had nothing to grieve about. He looked back on his life and reminded himself of all the pleasant memories: the time when he had a thousand dollars in the bank the dinners at the Japanese cafe where sake and pleasant banters with the waitresses brought a spirit of adventure to him. He remembered the woman on Post Street who had given him much pleasure. For a long while it had been his habit to spend his nights at her apartment. He remembered the musty autumn afternoon when she died. He recalled her face and figure.

It was many ages ago. Yes, his friends had settled down and brought up families. He remembered the trip back to Japan and the time he had spending all his savings. He came back to California flat broke. Yes, he had dined at restaurants, ate rich food and fancy dishes. Once he did own a car. It was at a time when very few Japanese had one. He had one then. Once, for a summer, money came in much too fast for him. He earned ten to eleven dollars a day that year. That was his earning peak, and he also recalled the scorching heat of that summer. Now that was long ago and he was in the city, on the second floor of an old boarding house.

Once or twice he opened his eyes and blinked at the light and made sure he was awake. He could clearly see that he had come along in the years. There was the present—the business of his life: the want ads, the ten cent meals, the bills, the debts, the unpaid rent, and his obligations. The loss of respect, the loss of honor. Finally sleep came and erased the earthly presence of the troubled mind.

He awoke early next morning. He went to the kitchen and found Mrs. Yamaguchi at the stove. Her husband was home. He was reading the morning paper at the table. It was his day off.

"Please, were there any calls for me this morning?" Gunsuke Iwamura asked the landlady.

"No. Not yet," she said. She looked at him observingly. "Did you have breakfast?"

"No," he said. "No."

"Sit down and have a cup of coffee," she said.

He hesitated. The woman's husband was looking at him. "Thank you very much," he finally said and sat down.

In the awkward silence he explained to the man. "I am waiting for a call from one of my customers. I like to stay here so I wouldn't miss it."

Mr. Yamaguchi nodded and went back to his paper.

"I put an ad in the paper for three days. I'm sure to get results today," Gunsuke Iwamura said.

The landlady smiled. "You will," she said. She brought him a cup of coffee and a couple of snails.

He ate silently and watched Mrs. Yamaguchi busy at the sink. Several times the husband went out of the kitchen to do errands. He went upstairs to open the windows of the vacant rooms. When he returned Mrs. Yamaguchi wanted him to bring up a bucket of coal. Once in the afternoon the man went out shopping to the market. When he came back he had a box of food for dinner.

Gunsuke Iwamura remained in the kitchen all day. He listened to the phone calls. Friends of Mrs. Yamaguchi called in the afternoon. One call was for Akira Yonai to contact Mrs. Anderson for daywork. Several were wrong numbers. He sat and waited. Sometimes he picked up Mr. Yamaguchi's papers and tried to read.

At supper time he went up to his room and waited till the dinner was over. He came down while Mrs. Yamaguchi was washing dishes. "Someone might call me at night," he explained to her.

The woman nodded. A little later her husband came in to warm himself by the stove. Every now and then he curiously looked at Gunsuke Iwamura.

At ten Gunsuke stood up. He couldn't go away without doing something for himself. He must do something. The intense gaze of Mr. Yamaguchi confused him. He recalled the name of his best customer. There was Mrs. Shaw. Surely she would hire him if she knew he was so hard up.

"May I use your phone?" he asked the husband.

"Sure. Go ahead," Mr. Yamaguchi said.

He tried several times. There was no answer. He went back to his seat. "I guess she's out," he said.

At midnight he stood up with a sick grin. Mr. Yamaguchi merely toyed with his papers and watched him. The man was waiting to see what he would do, what he would say.

"Think I'll turn in," Gunsuke finally said. "It's getting late."

In the kitchen Mr. Yamaguchi called his wife. "That means he will have no money coming in. Kick him out. We're not his relatives."

"Don't be too hasty," she said. "He's a fine man."

"You're too soft," he said. "We've been helping him for four months. That's too much. We cannot be fools. Pretty soon we'll be in the poor-house."

The husband went up to his room.

Mrs. Yamaguchi remained to rinse the dish cloth. As she finally wiped her hands with a dry towel she realized that she must face the issue. Sooner or later she must tell Gunsuke Iwamura to leave.

—1938

# It Begins with the Seed
# and Ends with a Flower
# Somewhere . . .

TWO O'CLOCK IN the morning. He is trying hard to sleep but is unsuccessful. The window shade is down and the room is dark. He switches on the light and the familiar objects of his room take shape. The chair, the table, the bureau. The reminders of his petty self and the run of his puny muscles. You are aware of the darkness outside, and the stillness of the yet unawakened energy of men and machines alike. You are in a hot bed with a pair of flighty hands and a heavy head. Your head is all right. You're not dizzy but you don't seem right. Always it came, he knew, after you had done your best with all you had, and yet failed, and your mother came after you picking you to pieces. Always it comes, he knew, when you are bewildered and lost, when you are hurt and there is no salve, when you leap up and in angry rushes slug the air, and cry and swear: I quit. I give up everything. The hell with it all.

He would like to get up and smash the chair into a hundred pieces. The table and the bureau too. All the familiar are hideous. God, take away my life and see if I care. Come doomsday. Let the war drums beat freely: I go willingly. I give myself for nothing. For honor, glorious death, and medals. Allow the fires of war to consume the routine of daily living. Shoot the fireworks here on my field. The field of lovely flowers, bah! Use my bones for a lighter and light up the flares of heraldry. Another man gives in! A cave falls; the mountains slide; the Ferry Building sinks several inches a year; an island disappears. I am through. Tom Sugimoto, operator of a nursery east of San Francisco, lays down his shovel. He's no good, I tell you. Putrid. Always a green-horn. Always a has-been. The grower of junk flowers. Buy my flowers, please. Buy my flowers, please. Good riddance!

Six hours ago it had happened. The last supper. This was the end. He did not know how many times it had happened before but a repeat he knew. When will this sinking feeling end and a new world begin? Where is confidence and nonchalance? Where is sureness? Ah, it is all over. Look at your hands. Is it not empty? Rejoice. Forget your shovels, your hoes, your hammers, and your trowels. Rejoice, for you gave in.

At supper the moments had come and blasted the schedule of his world. Long due it was but unexpected when it did come. Where did it begin? Where? Somewheres, Mother started to pop off, "Our plants are the worst-looking things of all the nurseries. They're sick and shriveled. What's the matter, Tom? Did you see Sato's carnations? No? Of course not. Run over there and see their carnations. Stems big as your thumbs, and flowers like our coffee saucers. Why don't you wake up, boy? Go out and see how the others grow them." A week before it had been Abe's sweet peas. The wonderful long-stemmed beauties of the market. Why don't we grow them like that? Why is it that ours are always short-stemmed with small flowers? Why do ours bloom when the market is flooded with sweet peas? There was always an answer. It was always this or that. There must be some means of an escape. Let me get a grip somewheres and hold on and get an ex-perience; let me have a faint hope . . . a toe hold. Not a total failure, please. Some encouragement, Mother. Please see where I stand. Please notice how I hesitate with growing bewilderment. Please do not rub it in. Look, as you say, at this sick-looking carnations of mine. It is my best today. I cannot do better. Please. It pains me to see someone spit on my plants. It kills me when someone interferes, and I am attempt-ing to prolong the sick-looking plants to old age.

But no. "Did you put in plenty of rawbone and rape seed last week?" "I did." "Go over and see how much the Satos put in each row. Just go over and see for yourself. Ours are the sickest-looking things in the whole town. Maybe you don't give enough water. Our leaves are thin and yellow. Go over and see how Sato's leaves spread out. Big and green giants. Come anything, is their plants' attitude. We're behind times. Ours are no good. You're no good, Tom." I am no good. I am worthless. I was the blame of it all. I am no nursery man. I am hope-less. The poundings of many hammers and the echoes of many wails.

The explosion of a mind without an outlet. The ripping of the nerves for relief. The all-the-way journey. I am through. I quit. The hell with it. For a dozen times: laugh, you are through. Cry, you are through. Rejoice.

Somewheres in the ancient times he had a confidence. Once upon a time a world of confidence. Watch me, Mother. Watch me grow things and make your eyes pop out. Watch me make you forget about Father. I shall plow the earth deep. I shall water all night long. Seeds, seeds, seeds, and cuttings. I shall study twenty-four hours. Seeds! I need more seeds. Spit on your hands. Get to work. First you screen the fine dry soil and fill up a hundred boxes. Water. Soak it through and through. Soak it three times. Careful. Sow the seeds evenly. Take your time. Go out and screen the soil finer for the top soil. Mix in the sand. Cover lightly. Get the sacks and cover the boxes completely. Go now and wipe your perspiration, and wait for the sun and the night to do their work. Ah, the seeds; the wonderful seeds. Not long ago he had a knack to do things right. The precise method of watering; the precise amount of fertilizer; the precise time of planting; and the precise intuition to disbud for a good season. Not long ago he had light feet and hummed the meaningless melodies. Not more than a week ago he had got a wit to drive on. My plants are not so good this year. What is wrong? I must find out. Yea, it was to come. Why did I not expect it with readiness? Where calmness? Where confidence? Where Mother? Not a total failure, please. See, I am breathing and living it out, and with the seeds I live and hope. Not the total thing, please. I know my plants are sick and shriveled. I know my soil is no good. It is used too often. I know I make many mistakes, but . . . . Ah, but rejoice. It is over.

Outside it is light. There is no sun and the air is cool. A faint hum of the motors on the highway seeps into the room. The sparrows on the trees are chattering. I was up earlier than you today. Sometimes in a vacant field you see a lone snapdragon plant shoot up and bloom for a long time in the hot sun. It is strong; it does not rot. There is no rust. Why? How? The wind carried the seed from somewheres; the dust settled over it; the earth gave warmth. Hew, man grower, effortlessly and skillfully. It begins with the seed and ends with a flower. Always it is so. Where is the difference between the non-grower and a man grower? Rejoice, Tom. It is not for you. What does it matter? Yesterday it mattered. The difficult problems . . . they were you. It is Tuesday today, and you are no more. You are free. Be glad. Sing; walk; play.

"Our flowers were terrible last year. Why don't our plants last as long as the neighbors? Can we call ourselves nurserymen? We're going to be the laughing-stock of the community. Fools we are." Rejoice. Sleep soundly, Tom Sugimoto. Relax, Mother. This is the day. Many holidays are coming, folks. Tom Sugimoto's carnations are drying up. Where's Tom anyhow? His plants in the back lot are crying for water. Has he forgotten them? What's happened to him? Where's Tom? I tell you, neighbors, I am on my way for a long vacation. Fishing? No. Hunting? No. I am covering the blanket over my head. Please do not disturb. Please, no more mention of seeds and flowers. Please. No, I. am not going to the flower market. Please, I don't want any fertilizer. I don't want sprays of any kind. Why, didn't you know? I am through. Sick? No, I am not sick. Broke? No, I am not broke. Yea, friends, I am through. That's all. Rejoice.

The sun is up. It is time to switch off the light. It is time for me to catch up with sleep. Good-bye, world. Good-bye, time. Pretty soon I shall need no calendar. Pretty soon I shall toss away my alarm clock. Noises in the kitchen begin. Must be around six. Mother is up. What for? What for on a day like this? Ridiculous of her to bother about a breakfast. Rejoice. Let a guy catch up with sleep. Let a guy escape in a dream or two. Who wants breakfast? I want nothing. What is that smell from the kitchen? Today is Tuesday. It is a mush day. It couldn't be pancakes. Boy, pancakes. It is not a pancake day. This is Tuesday. But . . . yea, the hot pancake smell. What's wrong with mother? This is Tuesday. Not the day for a stack of hot pancakes with butter, and syrup, and sweet youngberry jam, and a bowl of strawberries, and hot coffee. No. No, this is not the day. Today is Tuesday. But she is calling. "Tom! Tom! Breakfast is ready. Tom! Breakfast is ready." I will pretend not to hear. I will lie still and ignore her. Has she forgotten already?

She pokes her head in. "Tom. Breakfast is ready. Tom." She pulls up the shade and looks out into the field. Has she forgotten already? I needn't answer; I needn't answer. "Tom, Tom. Breakfast is ready. Hurry up or your breakfast'll be cold. Tom." I needn't answer. I want nothing. I am through. I quit. "Tom. Tom. Wake up."

I am through. I quit last night. The hell with everything. But I shall rise and eat breakfast. I shall go in as if nothing had happened. But I will not talk. I will sit tight and tackle the pancakes. Why should I talk? Has she forgotten about last night? When I am through I shall rise without a word and return to my room. "Tom. Tom. Hurry up."

Silence in the kitchen. Through the open window the shouts and the greetings of the neighbors come. The cars on the highway speed by. Somewheres a tractor is running. A crew of men picking cucumbers in the field. Mrs. Jones is hanging out her washings. A man in the distance is watching the brush fire. Our electric pump is going. Who started it? Mother is moving about swiftly and silently. Action. Silence. Seeds. I am eating full. Activity. All activities, and my silence, and my little world: I am through. I quit. The hell with it.

After breakfast he takes a walk. I am too full to sit around. Who started the pump? I will go and see if everything is okay. He walks unhurriedly. He does not leap. He does not sing. The familiar objects command attention. The red rubber hose. A box of broken glasses. A broken pitchfork. Empty carnation boxes. The trusty wheelbarrow. A faucet with a leak. On the way he looks at the back lot where the carnation plants are. The leaves look a bit soft. What is wrong? My plants are not so good this year. They look shriveled and weak. What is wrong? He walks over to the field and sticks his finger in the soil. Enough moisture. Better wait another day and water. What is wrong? What is wrong?

He forgets about the pump and turns back. He goes back to the house to fetch the package of snapdragon seeds for another try of a hundred boxes.

—1936

# III
# FAMILIES

# Miss Butterfly

THE DOORBELL RANG and Sachi ran nimbly to the floor. "Yuki!" she called to her younger sister. "I think they're here!"

"I'll be out in a moment," Yuki answered from the bedroom.

Sachi opened the door and found an old man standing on the porch. "Oh hello, Hamada-*san*," she said, her face plainly revealing disappointment.

"Good evening, Sachi-*chan*," greeted Hamada-*san*, entering the hall. "Is your father home?"

Sachi looked up and down the street and then closed the door. "Yes, Hamada-*san*. He's in the living room. Go right in."

The old man looked admiringly at her, pausing for a word with her. "My, you are growing prettier every day. Is Yuki-*chan* home too?"

She smiled and nodded. "We're going to the dance tonight with our boy friends," she added eagerly.

Hamada-*san*'s face fell but brightened quickly. "Do you still have those Japanese records—the festival music, I mean?"

"Yes," Sachi replied, looking puzzled. "We still have them."

"And is your phonograph in good condition?" he asked.

She nodded impatiently, anxious to return to her dressing.

"Good!" cried the old man, clapping his hand. "Please come into the living room. I wish to have a talk with you and your father."

"But I will be late for the dance!" she protested. "I must dress now."

Hamada-*san* looked pleadingly at her. "Please, Sachi-*chan*. Please, this is my special request."

The old man led her into the living room where her father sat reading the Japanese daily. "Saiki-*san*, how are you?"

Saiki-*san* dropped his paper and took off his glasses. "Good evening, Hamada-*san*. Anything new?"

Hamada-*san* dropped into the easy chair, leaning forward eagerly. "Saiki-*san*, I have one special request to make of your daughters tonight. It will bring me much happiness, and I shall forget that I am a lonely man for a short while. Please ask Sachi-*chan* and Yuki-*chan* to do it for an old man's sake."

"What is it you want?" asked Saiki-*san*.

"You may recall my repeated request in the past. I want to see the cherry blossom, the *taiko* bridge, and hear the Japanese paper houses hum when the wind blows. I want to dream of the pine-studded hills, the crystal-clear lakes, Fujiyama, Miyajima, and New Year festivals . . . the old Japan. My mouth waters with the flavors of the island fruits, rice cakes, and fish. My heart runs away with the color of the kimonos, the plaintive songs, and the loss of my many ancestors. Do you get it?"

Sachi groaned and waved her hands protestingly.

"So you wish them to perform Japanese folk dances," Saiki-*san* said, smilingly.

Hamada-*san* beamed and eagerly added," "*Odori*—that's what I mean. Please, Sachi-*chan*, wear your beautiful kimono tonight and perform one dance for me. Just one, that is all I ask. I want to capture my lost memories and dream. Dance for an old man and let him enter his old world for several minutes."

"No, I won't," she said emphatically, standing impatiently by the door. "I won't."

"Daughter, what are you saying?" Saiki-*san* said. "Make Hamada-*san* happy tonight. Wear your kimono and dance."

"One dance, Sachi-*chan*," begged the old man, humbly bowing. "For your father's old friend. He is poor and cannot reward you. Otherwise, he would shower you with gifts."

"I don't want anything," said Sachi, and looking at her father added, "I hate to wear kimono."

Hamada-*san* looked horrified. "Ah, Sachi-*chan*!" he cried. "Please do not say that. Don't you Nisei girls realize the truth? When you wear your bright, colorful kimono you are the most beautiful women in the world. Your eyes brighten up, your figure becomes symmetrical, your gestures move naturally. Don't you see, Sachi-*chan*?"

Sachi stood speechless, hesitating whether to laugh or smile.

"Sachi, why don't you like to wear kimono?" her father asked.

"It takes so much time, and I feel clumsy and stiff," she replied.

Hamada-*san* smiled and shook his head. "You don't look it when you wear it. You are merely saying that for an excuse. I don't believe it.

She looked at her watch and cried, "I've lost five minutes already."

"What time does the dance begin?" Saiki-*san* asked her.

"At eight sharp," Sachi answered eagerly. "Papa, may I go now?"

"Saiki-*san*! Please remember your old-time friend," cried Hamada-*san*.

From the bedroom came the younger sister in her glittering white evening gown. "I heard what you said about Nisei girls, Hamada-*san*," Yuki said, smiling. "Sachi, let's do one *odori* for him. It won't take but ten minutes, dressing and all, and it'll make him happy. I have your gown and the rest of your things out, all ready for you to slip them on."

Sachi though for a moment. "All right. I'll do it," she said suddenly. "Papa, please select the record and be ready when we come out."

"I'll do that," Hamada-*san* said, beaming. "Saiki-*san*, just sit and relax."

Eagerly he began sorting out the record albums. The girls rushed into the bedroom. After much deliberation the old man selected two records and went to the phonograph.

"This is my favorite," Hamada-san said to his friend, holding up one record. "This is about a day in autumn in Japan. The wind blows and the leaves fall. The sky is clear and the air is beginning to cool. The chants of the insects are dying out, and late harvest is about over. The flowers shrivel and the last of the leaves flaunt their brilliant colors in the wind, and the day awaits the icy blast of winter."

The girls' father sat silently, lit his pipe, and blew smoke. He watched his old friend poring over the words of another record and wished he had some kind of an answer for him.

"It's a beautiful piece," Hamada-*san* informed, indicating the first record. "Especially when dancers perform skillfully as Sachi-*chan* and Yuki-*chan*."

The two girls hurriedly skipped into the room. They wore their best kimono, a colorful design on silk, enhancing their youthful beauty.

"Are you ready with the music, Hamada-*san*?" asked Yuki. "We're all set."

At the sight of the girls in kimono Hamada-*san* sat up, his eyes wide with open admiration. "Beautiful, beautiful! The whole world should see you now."

Sachi laughed it off, and Yuki smiled happily. They went over to the phonograph and inspected the record. Satisfied with the selection they rushed Hamada-*san* to a seat.

"Sit down and enjoy yourself," Sachi said. "We'll watch the record. Hamada-*san*, there will be positively one performance tonight."

"Two?" the old man asked timidly.

"Positively one," Sachi repeated.

The music began, and the girls waited alertly for their cue. Hamada-*san* poked Saiki-*san* in the ribs as the two girls performed. He clapped his hands, keeping time with the music. His eyes, round with excitement, twinkled. His body swayed this way and that way. Then he forgot his friend, the time and place. Long after the music stopped and the girls paused by the phonograph, Hamada-*san* sat fixedly.

"Good night, Hamada-*san*," called the girls at the door.

"Wait!" cried Hamada-*san* springing to his feet. "Sachi-*chan*, Yuki-*chan*, one more! The parasol dance! Please, just one more. Please!"

The girls looked at each other, hesitating. Hamada-*san* ran to the phonograph and started record going. "Hurry, girls. Get your parasol!" he cried.

The high notes of a *samisen* and the mixed instruments cut the air. The girls ran to get their parasols. Hamada-*san* beamed and clapped his hands in tune with the music. Saiki-*san* sat comfortably in his chair, his eyes closed, and sucked his pipe.

The girls returned and instantly snapped into the dance. Their parasols opened and twirling, they leaped over imaginary puddles and worried about their slippers. They looked up at the sky, their hands out to see if the rain was falling. Their faces bright with smiles they twirled their parasols with happy abandonment. The sun is out once again, and they forget the puddles, the mud, and discomfort. Their bodies, minds, and hearts join to greet the sunny day, their somber aliveness increasing to gay abandon.

Once more Hamada-*san* sat motionlessly, unheeding the end of the music and the dance. Sachi stopped the phonograph.

"Wonderful! Wonderful!" cried Hamada-*san*, becoming alive. "I shall never forget this performance."

"Yuki, how much time have we?" asked Sachi hurriedly.

"Exactly ten minutes," Yuki said. "Let's hurry."

The girls dashed into their room.

"Wasn't it wonderful, Saiki-*san*? Wasn't it?" asked Hamada-*san*.

"Yes, they were pretty good," replied Saiki-*san*.

When the girls returned to the room their father was reading the paper. Hamada-*san* sat silently by himself in the corner, his eyes staring in the distance.

"How do we look, papa?" Sachi asked, the two girls showing off their new evening gowns.

"Swell," Saiki-*san* said, looking up.

"What do you think of them, Hamada-*san*?" Yuki asked old man. "Hamada-*san*!"

"Please don't ask me such a question, Yuki-*chan*. Not tonight," Hamada-*san* said sadly.

Sachi looked puzzled. "What's happened to you, Hamada-*san*? Are you ill?"

"Nothing is the matter with me. I'm all right," he said, cheering up with an effort. Then he added, "Sachi-*chan* and Yuki-*chan*, please be careful with your kimono. Don't let the moths get into them."

"We'll be very careful with them," Sachi promised.

"And don't you forget the *odori*. Keep brushing up."

The girls nodded obediently. Outside a horn blared.

"Oh, they're here!" cried Sachi, running to the window.

"Isn't it exciting?" Yuki cried, moving to her sister's side. "We're going to have a good band tonight."

The girls waved their hands, and the horn tooted again. "Good night, Hamada-*san*. Good night, Papa," they said.

"What is this dance? What kind?" the old man asked his friend, watching the girls skip out of the house.

"A social dance. Popular American pastime," answered Saiki-*san*, without looking up from his paper.

In the living room Saiki-*san* smoked incessantly and the place became stuffy. He continued to read the paper. Hamada-*san* sat mutely in the corner, his eyes smarting with smoke. He could have gone outside for a bit of fresh air but did not move. His eyes took in the phonograph, the record albums, the spots where the girls danced, and the room that was now empty. In the silence he heard the clock in the hall ticking.

—1939

# Between You and Me

Inside of a week we knew something was wrong at the Horita home. At first we could not tell what it was. The whole community was somewhat aware of it but could not come right out and say what it was. We could not figure it out for weeks. No one knew what was wrong at the house but perhaps the principals who did not reveal nor say a thing to anyone. The Horitas went about their work as usual. Nothing appeared to be wrong with them. Nothing was wrong outwardly but we could not get over our feelings that some unusual thing had happened at Horita's. We just felt it and thereafter took particular attention to the house; and there was something that did happen which was why all attention was focused on the Horitas.

When we sensed something was wrong at their house the folks went over a number of times to find out what was wrong and if possible to help. But it did not turn out the way the folks throught it would. The whole matter was impossible for solution and neighborly aid from the very beginning.

The Horitas do not care to discuss family matters or confide to the folks. They are known to cover and hide every movement of theirs so their intentions would not be known to the people and would be quietly and safely executed. The Horitas went about quietly through the years in the community and did not disturb anyone so they in return were left undisturbed by the folks. Father Horita ran a shoe shop on Eighth Street and his only son and the only child helped out at the store. They carried mostly cheap shoes in stock and rarely sold high-grade shoes. At the time when we sensed that something was wrong at their place, Father and Mother Horita were thinking of marriage for their Eiichi. They were probably thinking ahead of the time when Eiichi would take over the family responsibility and carry on. Also they were thinking of their own security and comfort in the old age. The fact that something might go awry and their plans might go haywire were the furthest thought of the Horitas and evidently they did not know what to do or how to handle such situations at a moment's notice.

When we sensed that something was wrong and went over to see the Horitas it was all over. I mean the happening, the matter which was causing anxiety and curiosity among us and perhaps sadness. When we went over to see what the whole matter was Father Horita came out and met us and talked politely just as in the times when we would go to see him about community donations and dues. He was a bit pale at the time but otherwise he was the usual self. Several times we expressed our fears of something unusual happening at his house but each time he shook his head.

"No, no," he said. "There's nothing wrong here."

So we did not find out directly.

For days we did not know what was the cause of our curiosity. Everything at Horita's looked all right. There was nothing wrong outwardly and about the only strange thing was Father Horita's paleness. He was usually red-cheeked. We lightly dismissed this strangeness; perhaps he was sick, perhaps he did not feel well. Finally we realized that we had not seen Mother Horita anywhere for days. We did not see her once on our visits to the house. We had not seen her anywhere for a long while. We became excited over the fact. The folks went about asking people if they had seen Mother Horita recently.

"No, no. Not for a long time," they said, and for awhile we were certain that something must have happened to her. "Maybe she is sick in bed or something," someone said. "No, this is more serious. She must have died or run away," another said.

Then one day someone passed the word around that she had seen Mother Horita at the market in town and looked the usual. Later several other folks reported seeing her so our hunch was over.

For weeks we got nowhere. Not that it mattered or concerned us but our curiosity got out of bounds and there was no stopping us. We got no help from the Horitas. We went about day after day and saw nothing. Just about the time when we were realizing our mistake in sensitivity, one of Eiichi Horita's chums came over to one of the neighbors' houses and talked. Inside of several hours we all knew Eiichi Horita was missing from home.

We learned right away that he had been missing for six weeks. "How stupid of us not to think of him!" we exclaimed among ourselves. Sure enough we had not seen him for many days. Perhaps this was not startling enough to us because we were used to missing him for a stretch of time.

Inside of a week we knew there were words between Father Horita and Eiichi and the son had left one late night without further trace. Although the Horitas did not know we knew, practically everyone in the community was familiar with the Horita affair. Over and over the folks talked about Eiichi and Father Horita and Mother Horita. As the saying goes, the quarrel was over a trivial matter. Almost everyone has long since forgotten what the argument really was.

Some of the folks insisted that business and money matters were really the cause of the quarrel. Some said Eiichi refused to marry Father Horita's choice which started them off to hot words, while others insisted it was merely a petty quarrel developing into bitter hatred. Whatever started the quarrel there was one authentic incident which everyone agreed as so.

In the heat of the quarrel, as one of Eiichi's chums was said to have heard from Eiichi himself before the disappearance, Eiichi stood up and faced his father. The son was pale with rage and when he struck his father's face he did not know whether he struck first or his father. Anyway with one blow upon the other the father and son parted away breathless and panting.

"I will go tonight!" Eiichi was said to have shouted. "I will go and never return!"

"Go ahead!" Father Horita had retorted. "Go ahead and don't return until you know how to talk to Father!"

Late that night Eiichi left the house without packing up. He wore a leather blazer and had sixty or seventy cents in his pockets. When he came down from his room he passed the living room where his father sat without a word. The father sat and heard his son close the front door, never to return, but did not move. Perhaps until that night it would have been ridiculous to suggest that such a situation would occur at the Horita home. Perhaps, as Eiichi's chum had often said, Eiichi did not want to leave home and town and the life he had lived so far but had to face Father. And perhaps the father too did not want his son to leave but defiance and the urge to crush his son's will got the better of him.

The whole affair was over many months later. It was a closed book to the Horitas as far as the community was concerned. We did not see Eiichi Horita again. The folks learned to take the Horitas in stride. We did not talk to them again about anything except how the weather was and about our health. And among ourselves we talked little of Eiichi Horita and began to lose ourselves in other interests of the community. Sometimes, however, we got together and talked and sooner or later the old topic came up: whether the neighbors had the right to forcibly butt into private affairs and perhaps be a nuisance and of service.

Meanwhile Father and Mother Horita still ran the old shoe shop. They get along by themselves in spite of old age and really have little to do with the folks. They go about their work as if nothing had happened in the family. In spite of old age they hurry and hurry and take no time to talk as the old folks do about the past or about Eiichi which makes us neighbors all the more sad and helpless. They go on dauntlessly and without much to say to anyone. In fact the Horitas have not as yet told anyone that their son was not living with them anymore.

—1940

# Through Anger and Love

FROM A PARKED automobile Haruo stuck his head out a little and peered across the street. Yes, he was still standing by the entrance talking to several men. His old man was talking and laughing as if nothing had happened yesterday. Had he forgotten already? No, his old man couldn't forget that easily. Haruo cautiously drew back and sat on the fender. Five minutes to seven by the City Hall clock. Promptly at seven, he knew, the flower market was going to open. What should he buy? What flowers were most popular, and most profitable? Suddenly he heard footsteps approaching the car. Instantly he was on his feet, and without looking back scurried around the corner. Safely past the corner he increased his pace. At a hundred yards he began to puff with exertion and slackened a bit. Just ahead he spied an alley and ran for it. Puffing and coughing he rested his nine year old body, his eyes trained on the sidewalk. Two minutes passed and nobody came after him. Slowly he came out and looked down the street and sighed with relief.

The market was open by now. Well, let the others go in first. He would walk around the block and take his time. Unhurriedly he stopped and looked at the store windows. Every now and then he looked up and down the street. Watching his chance he would slip in the market and make his purchase. He must look out for his old man. Then he must act natural when buying from the wholesalers so they would think that he was buying for his old man. Several minutes ago he was unsure of himself. He couldn't believe that he would be able to go through with it. Now he was sure of himself. He knew what flowers to get and where to get it from. His father bought a lot of things from Matsumoto and

Toscana. Matsumoto was a grower of carnations and Toscana raised roses. They knew him well. It would be easy. If only his old man would not appear at the wrong time.

Nearing the market once more Haruo slowed down. His eyes darted from the market entrance to the adjoining wholesale stores. Cautiously he stepped behind the row of parked cars watching for his father. He was not in sight. Should he take a chance now or wait awhile? He watched a number of people coming in and out of the market. Flower business must have been good yesterday. Almost all the florists were present. Should he hurry and buy before the flowers were all gone? Several more florists came out with armfuls of flowers. Haruo became desperate. He hurriedly crossed the street to a spot near the entrance. Growing bolder he peered through the window watching all sides, and then he saw his father.

His father was in the rear of the market purchasing cyclamen and mixed plants. He looked very much absorbed in the plants. Should he slip in now? Haruo could see Matsumoto whose table was near the entrance. At least he could get the carnations. Wait a minute. He became suspicious, cautious. Was his old man purposely in the rear so he would fall in a trap? Maybe his old man had seen him a few minutes ago and asked Matsumoto to look out for him. That would be terrible. Then he would have to go back home crawling on his knees. Undoubtedly his father would further humiliate him and kick him out of the house. Maybe Matsumoto did not know. He looked keenly at the carnation grower's face, watching for a tell-tale sign that he was looking out for his old man. No, he did not know. Matsumoto's face was calm and relaxed. His eyes did not shift about. Then he looked in the rear of the market watching for his old man. He was not around. He was gone. Eagerly he walked in heading straight for Matsumoto's table.

Haruo's face fell. Matsumoto's table was bare. Where did his flowers go? Did he sell out? He hesitated in his tracks. Matsumoto's eyes brightened.

"Hello, Haruo!" he cried. "How are you? My, you've grown. And how is your mother?"

"Fine," Haruo said hurriedly. He looked over the table. "Did you sell out? Have you any carnations left?"

"Do you want carnations?" Matsumoto asked. "Let's see. How many do you want?"

"Ten bunches," Haruo said eagerly.

The man looked under the table and started unwrapping a big bundle. "All right, Haruo," he said. "I'll give you ten. Mixed colors?"

"Yes, but give me lots of red."

Matsumoto laughed heartily and his belly shook. "You're a smart boy, Haruo. You know what sells."

Haruo looked about. Matsumoto laughed and talked too loud. He must get away. "Will you please wrap it up?"

"Are you going to take it with you now or your father is coming to pick it up?" he asked.

"I want it now," Haruo said quickly.

Matsumoto hummed a tune and took his time wrapping. Finally he handed over the package. "All right, Haruo."

"How much is it?" Haruo asked.

"Dollar and a half. I'm charging you only fifteen cents a bunch."

"Pay you next time," Haruo said.

"Sure. That's all right," Matsumoto cried, waving his hand.

Haruo fairly ran to Toscana's table. He must hurry. His father might return any minute. His eyes brightened at the sight of Toscana's good roses piled high on his table.

"Hello, boy," called the Italian. "Do you want to buy nice roses? I'll give you a bargain today."

Haruo picked up a bunch to see if the outer petals of the roses were bruised, and then satisfied examined the bases of the stems for the tell-tale mark of old flowers. Toscana chuckled and picked up several bunches for Haruo to examine.

All fresh flowers, my boy. No kidding," he said. "You want to buy for your papa?"

"How much?" Haruo asked hurriedly.

Toscana counted off six bunches. "Two dollars to you. A real bargain."

"I'll take it." He said quickly.

Haruo looked about while he waited for the man to finish wrapping. He must get away. Any minute now his old man would be coming back. Which entrance should he take, the front or the rear? Eagerly he accepted the package from Toscana.

"All right, boy," the nurseryman said, nodding and smiling.

With both arms loaded with packages Haruo walked off excitedly. He must hurry. He must catch a bus and ride back to his district and start selling his flowers. He quickened his little strides in the direction of the rear entrance. Suddenly from the front entrance came a familiar cry, "Haruo! Come back! Haruo!"

Terror-stricken he broke for the rear door. Gripping his bundles tight to his sides he ran past several tables unheeding the cries. Reaching the sidewalk he cut sharply to his right and then across the street. He must not be caught. It would be the end of him. He must get away. Running swiftly around the corner he headed for Seventh. He must shake his father off his trail. Should he go up or down Seventh? He must go up to reach the bus line, but suppose his old man was waiting for him at the next block? No, that wouldn't do. Should he run straight for First and wait around the pier, and later retrace his steps? That would be loss of time. No, he must go down Seventh and walk back to Twelfth. Then he remembered the jitney running on Seventh and his eyes brightened. His father would never think of the jitney.

To make sure his old man was not following, Haruo ran a couple of blocks more and headed for Sixth. At the corner of Sixth he sat puffing on the gutter looking in all directions, expecting the appearance of his father. Anxiously he looked to see if the flowers were bruised and the stems broken. They looked all right, and his anxiety turned to relief. He must sell them before noon while in good condition. In the afternoon they would start wilting without water.

Five minutes went by and his father did not appear. Cautiously he walked back to Seventh and waited for the jitney. Time after time he hid among the buildings whenever a figure appeared on the street. When the jitney came he boarded quickly and asked for a transfer. He slid low in his seat so he would not be noticed from the street. Several times the driver stopped the car for passengers. Haruo held his breath at every stop, expecting his father to jump aboard. At Clay the jitney turned left and passed Eighth, Ninth, and Tenth. He noticed the tall buildings coming into view. Three more blocks and he must get off and catch his bus. Maybe he should get off a block away and make sure his old man wasn't waiting at the spot. Scrambling to his feet he asked the driver to stop at the next corner.

No sight of his old man. He walked eagerly to the corner of Thirteenth and Clay for his bus. He wished the bus would hurry. Several minutes of waiting brought restlessness and uneasiness. Was the bus never coming? Then he caught sight of it in the distance. At last!

Safely on the bus and bound for his district Haruo leaned back with relief. His father would never find him now. With his feet on the front seat Haruo braced himself. His shoes did not reach the floor. Every now and then he looked into the packages to see if the flowers were all right. A dollar and a half to Matsumoto and two dollars to Toscana. He must pay them next time. He must sell pretty nearly all his flowers to make a good profit. He had ten bunches of carnations and six bunches of roses. That would mean twenty dozen carnations and twelve dozen roses. He must sell cheaper than his old man. How much should he charge? Twenty-five cents a dozen for carnations and thirty-five cents a dozen for roses would be a bargain. Anybody would buy at that price. First, he would go to the shops in the district that knew him. Mazzini, the Browns, Nick, Hamilton Hardware, Rosloff Service Station, Riley, Joe, and the rest. They were friends of his old man.

They would be glad to see him.

Haruo took out his pencil and pad and figured. The car moved and vibrated. Several times the flowers started to slip off the seat. Twenty dozens at twenty-five cents a dozen would be five dollars. Twelve dozen roses at thirty-five would amount to four dollars. Nine dollars for the day! That would be swell. He would give his uncle fifty cents a day for room and board.

The bus stopped and lurched. Haruo looked out of the window. Pretty soon he must get off. He put his pencil and pad in his pocket. He had better start selling right away. He must make good today. If he failed and had to go back begging for forgiveness his old man would laugh at him and give him a stick. No, he couldn't fail. When a boy has run away from home for good he should not think of going home. Even if it killed him he shouldn't. He should move on and take the consequences.

Gripping the packages tightly he waited for his block. Familiar buildings came into view. The Woolworth, Safeway, Gibson Drug, Palace Theater, Texaco Station, and Bank of America. His eyes brightened and he eagerly went forward to be let off. He could see Rosloff gingerly wiping a customer's windowshield. He could see that the Browns were doing a good business. He smiled. His hometown.

Haruo got off at the next corner. For a moment he stood bewildered and hesitating. What was his plan? Where should he go first? Again the dread of uncertainty and the fear of his future shook his nerve. Did he do right by leaving home? Was he at fault and not father? How did the quarrel begin? His cheeks burned at the thought of it. Last night his father slapped him in the face in front of his brothers and sisters and called him a fool. His brothers laughed and his sisters looked with astonishment. They saw him crying, and the hard shaking he got in addition. What did he do? He had done nothing. What was it? He didn't know. The quarrel began a long time ago. He must be bad, or his old man mistaken? Was it his quick temper or his father's? He leaned against the telephone pole wondering what to do. Suppose the folks did not want to buy flowers today? Suppose he couldn't sell enough to pay back Matsumoto and Toscana? He would be in a fix. He couldn't live at his uncle's any length of time without paying room and board. Then he heard Rosloff's familiar voice calling, "Hello there, sonny! Come over here!"

Haruo eagerly ran across the street, his packages dangling. "How are you, Haruo?" asked the service station man. "What you got there?"

"Flowers," Haruo said eagerly. "Carnations and roses. Would you like to buy some, Mr. Rosloff?"

He laid the packages on the ground and quickly unwrapped one of them. He held a bunch of carnations in each hand. "They're nice and fresh, and a bargain. Twenty-five cents a dozen."

The man laughed. "Come inside of the station," he said. "You don't want the sun on your flowers."

Inside his cool office Rossloff picked up red and white carnation bunches. "These are swell flowers."

Haruo nodded his head. He was busy unwrapping the other bundle. "I have some nice roses too. They're thirty-five a dozen."

"Are these your dad's or your own?" the man asked.

"They're my flowers. I'm selling them," Haruo replied.

"Your dad was here five minutes ago," Rosloff said.

Haruo looked quickly at his friend. He could not tell what the man meant by it. He kept still, busying himself with the flowers.

"I'll take a dozen of pink roses and a dozen each of red and white carnations," the man said. "I'm going to take them home and surprise my wife."

"Gee, thanks!" Haruo's eyes danced as he cut the strings of the bunches and started counting.

The man took a seat and examined a headlight globe. "You cut school today, Haruo?" he asked casually.

Haruo did not look up. He kept counting the flowers slowly. "Yes, I was busy this morning."

"You should be busy in school," Rosloff quietly said. "Let your father sell flowers and worry about money."

"I can't."

"Why?" The man carefully laid the globe on the shelf.

Haruo handed over the carnations and the roses to Rosloff. Hurriedly he wrapped his remaining flowers. "I can't tell you, Mr. Rosloff."

"Did you have a fight with your dad?"

Haruo nodded his head.

"Pshaw! That's all right, son. Forget it," Rosloff said. "Sometimes you've got to taste vinegar, and sometimes honey. That's the way it goes, Haruo, whether you're young or old."

He stood shifting his weight from one foot to the other.

"Oh, I forgot, Haruo. How much do you want?"

"Eighty-five cents," Haruo said.

The man opened the register and counted the money.

"Mr. Rosloff, please don't tell my father I was here," Haruo begged. "I've run away from home."

"I won't squeal on you," the man said. "You can depend on me."

Outside Haruo stepped along gingerly, his coins jingling in the pants pocket. Eighty-five cents to the good. A swell start. With luck he might make nine dollars. He hummed a tune. He'll show his father. This was his world. Why had he been afraid several minutes ago? He knew flowers. He liked flowers, Where did his fear come from? He laughed and wondered where to try next. Up ahead the Brown's two shops bustled with activity. Miss Brown's stationery shop always had customers. She was nice to everybody. He would go in there next. Maybe her father who ran a cigar-stand next door would also buy flowers.

Haruo walked in and found a lot of customers at the counters. Almost instantly he was the center of attraction. He smiled gratefully to Miss Brown who ordered him to open the packages. People cluttered about him. A lady wanted a dozen mixed carnations. One old gentleman bought two dozen roses. A young girl took a dozen carnations for her mother. Miss Brown purchased two dozen roses, and finally escorted him to her father's place. "Dad, why don't you buy some beautiful roses for mother?" she said. "He has some of the nicest colors."

Her father looked up from his work and examined the roses. He bought two dozens. Haruo walked away, his head high in the air. He chuckled and hummed. Flushed with confidence he went in Mazzini's, Hamilton Hardware, Riley's, and Joe's Garage right after another. When he came out of Joe's his packages were light. Four bunches of carnations and three bunches of roses left. His two pockets were bulging with small coins. How much had he made? He laughed. He must count the money. This was fun. Tomorrow he would take another portion of the town and keep rotating his route. He could go on forever. He smiled happily.

Haruo ran across the street to the park and sat under the shade of a tree. First, he tackled one pocketful of money and then the other. Three dollars and forty cents plus three dollars and sixty cents equals seven dollars. Seven dollars! He must have sold many dozens. Yes, sixteen dozen carnations and nine dozen roses. He could easily make nine dollars. He looked across the street at the bank clock. It was almost noon. His stomach felt empty. Nick's Cafe stood invitingly at the corner. Should he go in now and eat? He looked at the remaining carnations and roses. They were in pretty good condition. Yes, he could go in Nick's and eat and sell his flowers at the same time. He dumped his money in his pockets and picked up the flowers.

His hands bumped against the bulging pockets as he walked, and his thoughts returned to his triumph. Nine dollars gross profit minus three dollars and fifty cents cost equals five dollars and fifty cents net profit. He could do it. It meant freedom and pride. He could so as he pleased. On the way to Nick's he stopped short in front of a maroon Ford DeLuxe. It looked familiar. There was no one in it and he looked closely at the license plate. Quickly his eyes darted about the stores expecting to see his old man. His easy, springy stride of a moment ago became short hesitant steps. Somewhere in town his father was making his rounds. Where could he be? Suppose his father caught him by surprise? A look of terror crossed his face. He must get rid of his flowers right away and slip away from the district. Every few yards Haruo looked across the street and behind him expecting his father to jump out of hiding. Hurriedly he looked in Nick's. His father wasn't there. He felt hungry, he swallowed his saliva. He could go for three hamburger sandwiches, a pie, and a glass of milk. Cautiously Haruo stood at the corner and peered inside Nick's to make sure his father wasn't among the customers. Satisfied he crossed the street for Nick's.

At the doorway Haruo hesitated. Was he taking a chance? Suppose his father should come in while he was eating and grab a hold of him? His father would surely explode and soundly spank him in front of Nick and everybody. No, he mustn't take such a risk. First, he would go around the block and see if his father was in any of the stores. Then he would hurry back, order just a hamburger, and move on.

All around the block Haruo looked in every shop. He was sure that his father wasn't nearby. He broke into a run. Perhaps he could eat a piece of pie if he hurried. That would be swell. A banana cream or pineapple. He mustn't forget to ask Nick about the flowers. Maybe some of his customers would also make purchases.

Breathlessly he ran in the cafe and carefully laid his packages in the corner. First he saw Nick who broadly grinned at him. "Hello, young man!" he cried. "How are you?" Then he noticed his father sitting and facing him, his small gimlet eyes studying him with a sly smile. For a second Haruo stood open-mouthed and then backed away quickly to the corner to pick up the packages and run outside.

"Haruo!" cried his father, smiling and holding up his hand. "Haruo, come back here."

Haruo hesitated. His father was still sitting leisurely. He could get away easily. He could run out, hide, and never allow his father to touch him. There was danger in remaining. Still he hesitated.

"Come here, Haruo. How are you doing?" his father said. "Business good today?"

Haruo slowly approached his father. "I made seven dollars already," he said.

"Good! You're doing fine," his father said. "Sit down here, Haruo, and let's have lunch together."

"What'll you have, young man?" Nick asked.

Haruo sat down, looking cautiously at his father. "I want a hamburger and a banana cream pie," he said.

Nick went away to fill the order. His father looked in the corner.

"You still have some flowers to sell?" he asked.

Haruo nodded. "I have four bunches of carnations and three bunches of roses left."

"You sell them easily," his father said cheerfully. "Over seven dollars for the day. Not bad. I know you could earn it every day. You're pretty smart."

Nick came back with the order.

"Let's eat, Haruo," his father said. "I like Nick's hamburgers best. They're always good. How about you, Haruo?"

Haruo nodded his head while his mouth bit into the sandwich.

"I don't worry about you, Haruo," said his father. "No, sir. You can go out in the world today, and I know you can make a living. But your mama. She's worried about you. She wants you to come home. You don't want to worry her, Haruo."

Haruo sat silently munching his hamburger. He glanced at his father who smiled back. Nick whistled and watched the hamburgers sizzle in the pans. A noon whistle went off at the factory several blocks away. Presently people cluttered in Nick's. All around him Haruo listened to the talk of business and of labor. He listened importantly to their talk and watched his banana cream disappear.

"Anything else, young man?" Nick asked him.

Haruo smiled and shook his head. His father got up and paid the bill.

"Come home when you're through selling the flowers. Mama will be expecting you," his father said. "I have to go home now and watch the store. You take your time, Haruo."

His father went away. Haruo sat sipping his milk and listened to the men talking of inflation, civil liberties, and sports. When he was finally through with his lunch Nick came over and bought a dozen carnations. "Goodbye, young man," were the departing words of Nick.

Outside Haruo walked up and down the main street carrying his packages without attempting to sell a bunch. The sun shone brightly. This was a swell day. A swell day to go to the ball park and see the Oaks and the Seals tangle. No, it was a greater day than that. He could leap, sing, and run all the way home. This was something he had never before experienced. This was a great thrill. Then he remembered his greatest disappointment, bitterness, and loneliness of last night as a prelude to joy. His warm laughing face became solemn. Suddenly tears filled his eyes. He wiped his tears with his sleeves and wondered if the people were noticing him in such a condition.

—1950

# IV
# SEPARATE LIVES

# My Uncle in the Philippines

WHENEVER I THINK of my uncle in the Philippines I cannot believe he is dead. Perhaps I cannot get used to the fact because I've never seen this uncle of mine who had lived half of his life in the Philippines. I do not know how he looked except through a blurred photo which was taken years ago. Here I was born and raised in Oakland and having never left the California shore, I visioned the Philippine Islands as a dreamland. All that I've known him was through the tales of my parents and their village friends in America, and in these tales I used to visualize my uncle in the Philippines in a way which was beyond life and death, and flesh and reality. When the news came that he had died in Manila I could not place him as dead. I could see him plain as day walking about as when he was alive, and I could not be sad and overwhelmed by the news, and death, to me, looked a bit trifle.

This uncle of mine in the Philippines was the younger brother of my father's. My father left Japan quite early in his life for Hawaii but his brother who entered his manhood by attending the military academy, spent many years in Japan which was to influence his life. Although what he had done in Japan is of no concern of ours it may help us to see him as he really was in the Philippines, of which I and the family have no record whatever.

He was the one village folks referred to as "the most likely to succeed." There was no indication at the time as to what was to follow. He was simply brilliant and versatile. Actually he had done little to deserve any distinction except through what came naturally to him: sheer talent. He could do anything well. Everything he touched was exceptionally done. He could do a surveyor's work to a brown, compose *haikŭ*, paint, cook, teach, write Japanese characters like a master with brush and *sumi*. So he entered the military academy which was the beginning of his downfall and also the beginning of his journey out of Japan.

Ever since I could remember I was taken in by my uncle's prowess through the tales I've heard around the house. One time it would be my father recounting the old days. Another time my mother would be telling me what she knew of my uncle. Sometimes my parents' village friends would come to our house and reminisce. All in all, I gathered, this uncle of mine must have been somebody.

This was before I began to wonder why he was living in the Philippines. Why did he not stay in Japan and what happened to his military career? One day I asked Mother these simple questions and when she answered them in her direct, blunt ways, I really began to believe my uncle in the Philippines was somebody and had greatness in him although no biographer would look him up nor realize that he had existed once.

My mother had often told me since then that my uncle loved to drink *sake*. He did not drink to extremes and stagger about the house and the town but always liked to sit down at some cafe and quietly sip *sake* out of a little cup. When he was attending the military academy and was brilliant in his studies, he used to have special privileges to go into the town. On each occasion he used to slip in quietly and drink *sake* at some cafe. This was all right. Anyone could drink *sake* in Japan.

The whole trouble was that one day this uncle of mine ran up a bill at the cafe amounting to several hundred dollars. At the time he did not think very much of it. He could pay it out of his discharge bonus. If the cafe proprietor should lose faith in him and demand immediate settlement he would write to his eldest brother who had a big farm to help him out. He would settle the bill for him. My uncle was certain of it. But if his brother should refuse this time, he could always resign from the academy and receive a lump sum of several hundred dollars with which he could pay the bill. So he wrote his brother asking for money, telling him that if he should not be able to pay the bill, he must resign from the academy as soldiers who run up debts and cannot pay must resign or be dismissed.

My mother was at his brother's farm at the time when the letter came. When the brother read the letter he could not work all day. "He was furious," my mother said. "He said, 'What does he think I am? Paying his tuition, supporting him so he could rise high! The nerve of him asking for money for pleasure's debts! I am no fool! Let him do as he pleases!' "

And my mother hearing the outburst begged him to give his brother one more chance. "Think of all the things he loses," she had said. "All his time and energy would be lost . . . and his talent."

"He should have thought of it long before this," the older brother had said. "Let him do as he pleases now. Not a *sen* more!"

Not a week later my uncle who was doing brilliantly at the academy was back home, having resigned and paid his debt. With the military career at an end he should by rights have been squelched and sunk to a drunkard, visiting the local cafes, doing the rounds as he pleased without a curfew to bother him. But he didn't sink. Perhaps he was never meant to be a drunkard. Anyway he began to teach school. Teaching school was easy for him. He taught school in the daytime and still had time to spare. At night he read a lot. He read books on philosophy and literature. However my uncle did not stay long a teacher. My mother always took pride in telling about the time my uncle applied for a surveyor's job on a government project.

"Think of it," Mother used to say. "Your uncle ranked second in the examination out of five hundred applicants. He was a man."

The work was to take him into Korea. Before he sailed he did something which came and was done. I do not know for sure whether it was his oldest brother or the family who arranged the marriage for him but at least, I know it was arranged. My uncle that year married a village girl whose parents looked upon him as promising. When the young couple sailed off to the new lands of Korea it was also their honeymoon. My uncle worked there a year. Perhaps he might have stayed in Korea and rose high as a surveyor but this he could not do. His young wife did not like Korea. She was homesick and a year away from home was too much for her. So my uncle and his wife left Korea and good pay for home.

Once back in the village of Hiroshima, Japan, the future began to tell the fortunes of my uncle's. He sat all the time at her parents' home, doing nothing but read. My uncle always did like to read so when he saw his chance of reading more books he took it. He did not search for jobs. He could have easily found one. And when the parents of the girl saw my uncle lying around the house, doing nothing but read, they became afraid and talked about divorce to their little girl.

When this uncle of mine finally sailed for the Philippines he was divorced. As to what he did in the Philippines the rest of his life there is little record and is of little importance. He did not become great. Later we found out that my uncle had settled down in Manila and opened up a merchandise store and did fairly well. He remained single the rest of his days. He rarely corresponded with his relatives.

My father did not write to him. All he knew was that his brother was somewhere in Manila, perhaps dead, perhaps long lost in drink and dissipation, perhaps unheard and unknown to the Japanese in Manila. At one time our family had the impulse to write a letter to the Japanese Association of Philippines, asking the whereabouts of my uncle. We did not write the letter which was the ironic part of it.

When the news came from Japan that my uncle in the Philippines was dead, we immediately came in touch with my uncle's associates in Manila. Days later my uncle's associates wrote to us about my uncle in the Philippines. He was a fine upstanding man of the community, they said. He was the president of the Japanese Association for fifteen years if that was anything. They have built him a fine monument in memory of him. My uncle's friends were kind enough to send us his pictures and the photograph of the monument. And also with the letter came my uncle's writings and sketches. Perhaps we would like to look over them. My uncle sat up nights alone, they said, and wrote them.

Today, years after death, we open up the old trunk where documents and papers are stored and take out my uncle's writings and sketches. Perhaps they are valueless; I do not know. I could not read his *haikŭ* nor understand his drawings so the value of them does not bother me. The family feels the same way about it.

We sit and sometimes talk about my uncle as if he was still walking about, pacing in his room behind the store and also composing and sketching. We could see him pouring himself cups of *sake* just as he had been doing all his life. We could see him lying around the place reading books on philosophy. At least, I could not believe he was dead. Even with the help of the picture of his monument I could not believe it.

In the winter when the evenings are long the old village friends come to visit my parents. They like to talk of the old days. Sooner or later my uncle in the Philippines becomes the topic of our talk. Perhaps when the old village friends die one by one and come no more to our house and my parents also die, we shall forget there ever was a man like this uncle of mine. Perhaps his life is not colorful enough and in time he will be buried under the many millions of deaths. But his life deserves more than a space in the obituary notice. Some day when our family can afford it we are thinking of publishing a book of his poetry and paintings, regardless of its value, and do our bit to resurrect immortality, not merely for the sake of my uncle but for the likes of him.

—1941

# The Loser

ORDINARILY SHE WOULDN'T think of walking fourteen blocks for anything but today she was punishing herself. She could have easily borrowed carfare from her son and saved some time. Halfway to the bus station she stopped to catch her breath. She was gasping and perspiration dripped from her face and neck. What a fool. "What made me forget my handbag?" she said to herself again and again. She had clutched it to her side all the way from Los Angeles and relaxing like a fool at the station she had laid it on the bench. The thought of her lifesavings in the bag gnawed her insides, and she picked up her brisk pace unseeming for her age. She counted the money in her mind— $3510 in bills and a few coins.

If I'd only find it. If it's still there, she thought. The money was the only reminder of her hardworking years. Thirty years of houseworking, foregoing necessary items, had built up the savings, and now in a foolish slip of a moment she had lost it.

The bus station came into view and her hope rose. She remembered sitting at the edge of the last row. There was no one near her bench. Maybe it was still there unnoticed. She fairly ran the last block and made straight for the bench. She almost stopped breathing to realize that the handbag was gone. After a moment of relapse she scrambled about, looking under the bench and asking people standing about. The handbag had disappeared.

Dashing to the clerk at the counter she told him of her loss. The clerk was sympathetic but had no knowledge of the missing bag. He was busy directing the traffic but noticing the crestfallen figure of the old woman he said, "I'll do what I can. I'll notify the police."

91

He took her name and address, the description of the bag and its contents. As she waited for the clerk to contact the police, she thought of her imminent situation. She would now be a burden to her son. She wished so to be independent. She had counted on her savings to see her through the rest of her life. If I had the money back again, she thought, I'd give half of the amount to the finder. She wondered if there were any honest people left in the world.

Then she heard the clerk calling her. He was holding the line as he explained the good news to her. A man had just come to the police station with her bag and money. "Tell the police to hold the man," she cried happily. "I want to reward him for his honesty."

In her excitement she forgot to thank the clerk for his trouble. She hurried toward the address of the police station. I'll give him five hundred, she thought. I'm lucky that an honest man found my handbag.

Her legs began to tire now and the ache in her left ankle reminded her past year. It had bothered her last winter, costing her two hundred in doctor bills and lay-offs. She wondered if the ankle would give her trouble this winter which would mean added expenses. Perhaps she ought to give the honest man a hundred and keep the rest for safekeeping.

As she neared the City Hall which was her destination, she began to think of her son and his family. He wasn't doing so well in his grocery business so she should pay her room rent. One hundred dollars would almost cover a year's rent for her. In her mind she rolled over and over the amount. Yes, a hundred would be too much for a reward—even for an honest man. Twenty dollars would do.

Walking up the steps of the building, she chuckled with glee, relief written over her face. The money was safely hers now with the police holding it for her. After several inquiries she went to the right office. On the way, however, she heard police calls which reminded her that she must get herself a small radio for her room. She should not, she reasoned, use her savings for luxuries but a radio she could not do without. Finally she made up her mind. The man will be rewarded ten dollars. He shouldn't be expecting a reward from an old woman. Ten dollars would express her thought as much as a twenty.

The police and the man were waiting for her. After she correctly identified her handbag, the police released it to her custody. Immediately she began counting the money, partly to reward the man and to see if all of her savings were there. She counted twice to see if she had made a mistake. After the second counting, she gazed at the man who had found her bag. The man was smiling but he appeared to her as the kind who was too smart.

"Where did you find the bag?" she asked the man.

"On the street, ma'm—San Pablo." Noticing the woman's troubled expression, the man said, "Anything wrong?"

"There's ten dollars missing. I had $3510 and a few coins when I lost the bag. Are you sure you didn't look inside my handbag?

Patiently the man admitted, "I looked inside the bag, yes, but I didn't take any of your money. I just looked for your name and address."

She was insistent. "But ten dollars is missing."

The man shrugged his shoulders. "And I didn't take it."

The officer said, "Look, lady. Aren't you glad enough to get the bulk of the money back?"

"Ten dollars is missing," she said. Now the man, to her, was the kind who would take the money. "Officer, he should be arrested for stealing."

The officer said, "Lady, there's no proof that he took the money."

"I'd like to have him searched, officer," she said.

The man laughed but his face was serious. "Okay," he said. He emptied all his pockets, turning them inside out, and put its contents on the desk. There was the usual wallet, keys, cards, matches, and a pen. The man opened his wallet and took out the bills. "I have three dollars and fifty-eight cents, and they're mine."

A moment later the police dismissed the case. All the way back to her son's house, she kept thinking about the man who had found her handbag. She was certain that the man had stolen her missing ten dollars. Now she would have to forego, she realized, the luxury of new reading glasses to relieve her of headache.

—1953

# Four-Bits

THE ROOM WAS filled and the men went about looking up their acquaintances. They stood in groups waiting for Joe Rugg to return and start things going. The early ones were already seated at the tables talking and smoking. The place was stale with smoke, a sign of absence of women. Every now and then the waiters came in to see about serving the food. Time after time the men dropped nickels in the phonograph, and the music, the shouts and laughter reigned in the room.

At one of the corner tables sat two young men enveloped in their little world. Things were different for Tad Yama and Johnny Blake now that they had met again. To others it was just another stag. To them: a reunion, mingled with memory and friendship. Not long ago they had seen the games together, studied the same books, and secretly admired the same girls. They had been together for years, and then one night with a diploma they were pushed out into the world. Here they were, after a lapse of relationship, safe and sane. Johnny Blake was now slightly bald, and Tad Yama wore glasses. But the two overlooked such a little matter as outward change and picked up the threads of the old days.

"Been a long time since we last saw each other," Tad Yama said, smiling. "Is it ten years?"

"That's right, Tad. Ten years," Johnny Blake said. "Ever been back to the old school?"

Tad shook his head. "I keep wanting to go back and never do."

"I wonder if Munson's still teaching English," Johnny said. "I clearly remember the old gang. Ed McGee, Lee Hoy, Sam Herman, Tony Olivera, Evelyn Dale, Fat Schultz . . ."

95

"Evelyn Dale—what happened to her?" Tad said, his eyes lighting up.

Johnny Blake glanced at his friend and looked away. "I don't know," he said.

"Did you lose track of her too?" Tad said, smiling.

Johnny grinned and nodded his head. "The good old days. I'm a funny guy. I want to keep my memory a dream and yet I want to develop it."

"Evelyn was beautiful," Tad said.

"She still is, I'm sure," Johnny said quickly.

A commotion rose in the room.

"Joe Rugg's back," Tad said. "I guess we'll eat now."

Johnny looked in the direction of the entrance and waved as he caught Joe Rugg's eye. "Good old Joe Rugg," he said.

The men took their seats and the waiters came in with their trays of soup and salad. Tad beamed at Johnny and the latter looked curiously.

"The last time was at the school cafeteria," Tad said.

"With hot dogs, milk, tamale, ice cream and chocolate bars," said Johnny.

Joe Rugg came around patting each man on the back. Across the table from Johnny one of Joe's friends shouted, "Hey, Joe! Don't forget we paid five bucks apiece. I want my money's worth."

"Don't you worry, Red," Joe Rugg called back. "Wait until you see the girls come out and do their stuff."

"They'd better be good," Red cried jokingly.

Joe came over to Johnny and Tad. "Break it up, you guys. This is a party," he said, laughing.

Johnny playfully punched Joe on the arm and the latter ruffled Johnny's hair.

"Have a good time, boys," Joe said.

"Sure, Joe," Tad said.

Red stood up and leaned over the table. "Hey, Joe," he said. "Is it on the level about the girls? How many did you rake up?"

"Four peaches—and they're good. Wait'll you see them," Joe said.

"They'd better be good," Red said and sat down.

Johnny looked at Tad and laughed. Joe Rugg went away shaking his head. For a while Red sought his neighbors' attention.

"Where are you going after finishing here, Johnny?" Tad asked, ignoring Red's funny cut-up.

"No place. Why?" Johnny said.

"Let's take in other places. It's early," Tad said.

Johnny nodded his head. Red quieted down and the two friends ate leisurely, lost again in their mutual world.

"Tad, you used to always talk about going to college. Did you go?" Johnny said, his eyes heavy with wine.

"No, I've never seen the inside of a college," said Tad. "My father had bad luck and I had to go to work. I'm a gardener now. What do you do, Johnny?"

"I'm a bookkeeper," Johnny said.

"Good," Tad said.

"Good? What's good about it?" asked Johnny. "You know what I wanted to be. A reporter on a big city daily, and I'm still on the lookout for a job."

Tad grinned. "Something may come along any day."

"I wish the show would start now so we could get away early," Johnny said, looking about the room. "Everybody's through eating."

"Here come the waiters to clean up," Tad said. "What are the girls going to do? Sing and dance?"

"You know Joe Rugg," Johnny said. "He likes the kind who'd do the strip-tease like in burlesque. You can bet on it."

Tad laughed. "He has company tonight," he said. "Say, Johnny, are you married?"

"No, Tad. Are you?"

"No," Tad said. "I haven't saved enough to marry."

"And I haven't fallen in love. I don't know why. I should and I haven't," Johnny said.

The tables were soon cleared and the waiters went about picking up stray napkins and cups. Red stood up and shouted across the room, "Hey Joe. How about starting the show?"

Joe Rugg nodded his head and waited for the waiters to finish up so they could leave the room. When the waiters left Joe locked the door. The men started to clap their hands, and finally Joe started things going by introducing a couple of girls. They sang and played the piano. Johnny and Tad applauded and entered into the spirit of the room. Red shouted that he wanted something hot, and the men laughed and shouted their approval.

Joe Rugg held up his hands. "Hold on a minute," he shouted, chuckling. "Something's coming up, men. Next we'll have strip numbers by four girls. Let's give 'em a hand."

A blonde came out first in a long evening gown and danced about the room. She proceeded to strip off her gown amidst the men's ejaculations and wound up in the corner of the room in her shorts and bra. A generous applause followed. She came out again and this time promptly discarded her bra. The men whistled, clapped hands, and shouted encouragement. She went around the room and, once again, ended her strip in the corner by taking off her briefs. Encore after encore the blonde was brought back in the room, and she willingly returned to please the audience but did not take off her only covering, a silver-painted leaf.

"More, more," cried Red, shouting himself horase. The others took up the cry, "More! We want more!" The blonde came out again and again. "Take it off. Take it off," Red cried. She did not take off her leaf. Johnny winked at Tad, and the latter shook his head smilingly. As if to appease the men the blonde appeared again and went about the room sitting on men's laps. To several she laughingly offered her breasts, and when their hands came up to paw she slipped away and continued her dance.

"Give her a rest," shouted Joe Rugg, breaking up the encore. "There are others, men—three more. Let's go around first. Remember, we have all night."

A moment later the second girl came out to do her stuff. She was a tall brunette with a nice figure and came out in a bra and a pair of flimsy tights. She danced smoothly, her movements of strip-teasing attuned with the music. When the girl approached the table where Johnny and Tad sat Red whistled loudly and long. For a moment she faltered. Johnny looked at Tad, and the latter looked at the girl and back to his friend. Do you see what I see? Johnny's eyes asked. It must be her. She is Evelyn Dale, Tad's eyes said. The brunette's eyes were centered on Johnny and Tad. For a second a twinkle of recognition entered her eyes and then disappeared. Her cream-white skin turned pink. Johnny and Tad did not watch her wind up her dance. Men shouted encouragements. Evelyn—Evelyn Dale, Johnny's eyes slowly said as he sat stiffly and watched Tad. She capped her dance by flinging off her bra and shimmying her body.

Across the table Red loudly clapped his hands and stuck his fingers in his mouth and whistled. Others followed it up and the room became noisy again. "More, more!" Red cried. She came out smiling, wearing tights. Johnny and Tad studied her closely, as if to reassure themselves, when she came around to their table. She was still smiling, a half-defiant sort of way, with none of her previous faltering movements.

"Stick around here for a while, baby," Red shouted at her.

She threw a big smile and circled about their table. The girl began the process of discarding her tights in front of Johnny and Tad. Red whistled. "Atta, baby!" he cried.

When she finally left their part of the room Johnny stared at Tad. They did not look at her again. She did an encore and followed with another. She received an ovation.

"Let's beat it," Johnny said to Tad, rising.

Tad stopped him. "We can't go just now, Johnny. Wait'll the show finish."

Two more girls followed with similar dances. Encore after encore followed, and laughter and encouragements filled the air. Several minutes later all the girls returned to their dressing room, through for the night. Several men stood up to go. "More, more! We want some more," Red kept yelling. Finally he went over to Joe Rugg's table.

"It's all over now, Johnny. I think we'd better leave," Tad said, rising.

"Okay, let's go," Johnny said quickly.

Johnny and Tad, along with several men, started for the door when Red and Joe Rugg rushed over.

"What's the rush, boys?" Joe Rugg wanted to know. "Stick around."

"We're going home, Joe. It's all over, isn't it?" Johnny said.

"The hell it is," Red cried. "You go over, Joe, and talk to the girls. I'll hold this bunch in the room."

Joe walked off to see the girls. Red gathered the bunch around him. "You guys are crazy leaving so early. Be wise and stick around," he said. "Listen, you guys. The girls are willing to come out here naked for four-bits apiece. You want to miss it? For four-bits, boys— wake up."

The group was silent. Finally Johnny nudged Tad. "I guess we'll go, Johnny," Tad said.

"Don't be a piker, Johnny," cried Red, holding Johnny's arm. "Look at those men at the table. Not one of them leaving but you bunch. Come on. Don't spoil the party."

Joe Rugg came running over. "Get back to your seats, boys," he cried. "One of the girls is willing for four-bits. Hurry up, Red, and get a couple of men to pick up the money."

Red pushed the bunch back to the tables. Johnny and Tad went back to their seats.

"What did we come here to celebrate?" Tad said, looking slyly at his friend.

"We're here because we bought tickets from Joe Rugg and Joe is our customer," Johnny said. "Right?"

"Right," Tad said.

A man came around collecting the money. The girl who played the piano all evening came back. Red returned to his seat and winked at Johnny and Tad. Joe Rugg signalled, and the piano music arose above the noise.

The room became suddenly silent and Evelyn Dale appeared wearing a fur coat. A thunderous applause greeted her. She went over to the piano and tossed her coat on top of it and whirled around, standing naked before the audience with a smile.

Red's familiar whistled came over the noise of other men. "Boy, look at that fuzz on a peach," he said.

She began to dance. She snaked in and out from the tables, slowly circling the room. "Where did you leave your leaf, Evelyn?" a voice addressed her from the audience.

"Here in my hand," she said, laughing. "Do you want it?"

"Sure, sure! Give it here!"

She tossed the leaf in the air, caught it deftly, and tossing back her head started trucking.

Johnny sat staring ahead, averting Evelyn. Red noticed it. "Wake up, Johnny. Look at the fuzzy-wuzzy coming."

Johnny sat motionless.

"Don't you want to see the box, kid?" Red said.

"No," Johnny said.

Red shook his head, his eyes returning to the girl.

Several minutes later her dance ended with a wild applause. Some men stood to get a last glimpse of her. She came back for an encore. Twice, three times she returned with the unending approval of the crowd.

"Come on, Tad. Let's get out of here," Johnny said at the first chance.

Tad followed after his departing friend. Not until they had walked several blocks did Johnny slacken his pace. After a while his taut figure loosened up a bit and his mouth lost some of its sullenness.

"Well—the old Evelyn is dead," he said.

Tad looked at him. "The world's full of new Evelyns, Johnny," he said.

The sky was heavy with dark clouds and the streets were deserted. A few taxis waited on the corner for the late ones.

"I'm chilly. Let's get a drink some place," Johnny said.

"All right," Tad said. "That'd be swell."

"I'm not sore at her," Johnny quietly said.

"No sense getting sore at her," Tad said. "She's not dirt."

"Let's go to Tiny's," Johnny said, more cheerily. "Have you been there recently?"

"No. Let's go to Tiny's," Tad agreed, and the two stepped briskly up the darkened street.

—1938

# V
# CONVERSATIONS OVERHEARD

# Oakland, September 17

THE THREE OF us sat and talked. An hour ago we did not know one another. The young Japanese girl was sitting at a table at Tabe's Fountain when I walked in. A little later a young Japanese in blue sweater and cords came in. We were tending to our own business when all of a sudden the fountain attendant dropped a glass of water and broke it into many pieces. That was the beginning of our conversation. It loosened us into friendly smiles and talks. At first we talked to the attendant. Each one of us said it was too bad. A little later we began to talk among ourselves. The young Japanese in blue sweater and cords and I went over and sat at the girl's table.

"My name is Jiro Hageyama," said the young man in blue sweater and cords.

"And my name is Hisashi Satow," I said.

The girl smiled. "My name is Barbara Akita," she said. "I am on my way to New York."

We shook hands and sat down. "So you're on your way to New York," said the young man named Jiro to the girl.

"Yes," she said. "In a few hours I will board the train and say goodbye to Oakland."

"Do you live in Oakland, Miss Akita?" I asked.

"Let's not be formal," the girl said. "My name is Barbara."

"All right, Barbara," I said. "Do you live in Oakland?"

"No," Barbara Akita said. "I came to visit San Francisco before heading for New York."

The young man named Jiro clucked his tongue and shook his head. "I wish I could go to New York. I know I'll never have the chance."

"You are too young to talk like that. There is still time," Barbara said.

We called the attendant and ordered three Coca Colas. Every now and then Jiro Hageyama looked outside. It was still light outside.

"I have a truck parked out there," he explained. "Once I got a ticket here for overparking."

We laughed. The attendant brought the Coca Colas. Barbara Akita looked at her watch. "I see I still have time to spare," she said.

"When is your train leaving?" Jiro said.

"Seven forty-two tonight in Berkeley," she said.

"You have lots of time," I said. "Let's go somewhere and eat."

"That's a good idea," Jiro said. "I know a good chop suey house on Eighth Street. We'll go there."

We came out of Tabe's and immediately went to the chop suey house on Eighth Street and took a booth. "This is something I'll remember in my old age," Barbara said. "When I get married in New York I will be tied up thereafter."

"Are you going to New York to get married?" Jiro said.

"Yes. Exactly," Barbara said.

"Where are your parents? What are you doing here in Oakland?" I said.

Barbara smiled. We watched her smooth back her silk-black hair. "My parents are waiting for me in Denver," she said. "My home is in Denver. Before I marry I wanted to come to the coast for a visit, especially San Francisco and the Bay Region."

"You're a Denver girl then," Jiro said. "I'm a Salinas boy."

"You are!" Barbara said. "And you, Hisashi?"

"An Oakland boy," I said.

"Then that's all settled," Barbara said.

"You must know your future husband pretty well," Jiro said. "Denver and New York is pretty far apart for a Japanese."

"On the contrary. I do not know my fiancee very well," Barbara said. "I met him once at home. That is all. Our marriage was arranged by our parents."

"A *baishaku* marriage for you!" Jiro said. We laughed and Barbara joined us. Jiro continued: "Fancy a girl like you coming unchaperoned to the coast who has her marriage arranged by the parents."

"Just the same that's how it is," Barbara said.

"Perhaps you love him.. Love at first sight," I suggested.

"I can't say I love him," she said. "I do know I don't hate him."

"Why did you consent to such a marriage?" Jiro asked. "You should have waited and picked someone of your own choice."

Barbara smiled. Her fingers toyed with a teacup. "You're not a girl so you don't understand," she said. "A Japanese girl can't wait too long for a marriage. She must think of her age. My parents became worried and their friends arranged my marriage."

When the food came we ate. We talked of other things.

"You must have enjoyed visiting California. You must have friends here," Jiro said.

"No, I have no friends here," she said. "I was pretty much alone. I went about alone. I enjoyed myself though. I went to the museums, the art galleries, the beach, the zoos, Golden Gate park, the ocean. I went to see the ocean almost every day."

"Too bad we didn't meet you sooner," Jiro said. "You should have seen the Yosemite at least once."

"I am perfectly contented," Barbara said.

"And now you are ready to meet marriage," I said.

Barbara smiled. "Yes," she said.

Although the dinner was finished we sat around and talked. Barbara looked at her watch. There was still time. One hour and fifteen minutes. "And now may I ask you some questions?" she said.

We laughed. "Go ahead!" we said.

"Jiro," she said. "If you are a Salinas boy what are you doing here in Oakland with a truck?"

"I'm a truck driver, Barbara," Jiro said. "Several times a week I come in with produce. Today I brought in a truck-load of lettuce."

"How interesting," she said. "Do you like the work?"

"I like it and hate it too. It's pretty dull. Sometimes I want to get away and roam."

"At least you do much traveling in your work," Barbara said.

"Yes. Back and forth and in circles," Jiro said.

"I believe we all do," she said. "And you, Hisashi? What do you do?"

"I raise flowers," I said. "I have a nursery where I raise carnations and snapdragons and pompons for the market."

"How fascinating!" she said. "That is a beautiful life."

"It's work," I said. "However, I like it better than being in business."

"Don't you like business?" Barbara said.

"No," I said. "I hate it from experience."

"My," she said. "We are getting to know one another pretty intimately."

Ten minutes later it was time for Barbara to go. We got up and before I knew it Jiro had paid the bill. "Say," I said.

"Don't make a scene, old man," Jiro said. "Forget it."

"All right," I said. We got out in the street and the lights were on. It was dark now.

"Let's see Barbara off," I said to Jiro. "We'll go in my car to Berkeley."

"Sure," Jiro said. "Barbara, we'll see you off."

"That's awfully nice of you, boys," Barbara said.

"How is your baggage arranged?" I said.

"It was sent ahead," she said. "I have several suitcases at the hotel."

"Do you really must go tonight, Barbara?" I asked.

She nodded. "My parents have my wire. They'll be expecting me on time."

When we reach the Berkeley station we had very little time to spare. There was time enough to shake hands and say goodbye. We saw her off a minute later. She leaned out of the window and waved to us when the train began moving.

"Goodbye, New York," said Jiro. "Goodbye, New York," I said.

"Goodbye, Salinas and Oakland," she said. We smiled.

She looked very attractive. The fact that this was the last I would ever see her made her very beautiful to me. A moment before we were talking and laughing together. She looked very small and helpless. She was going into it cheerfully. For a moment I wished I could leap on the train, reach her and unsettle her life. "Stay, Barbara," I'd say. "Stay here." It would be wonderful. For a moment I thought it would be wonderful. She would stay, she would live here. For what? Then I knew I was helpless and there was nothing I could do.

Afterwards I drove Jiro back to Oakland.

"I guess I have to be getting back," Jiro said. "Tomorrow I must work in the fields."

"Let's meet again, Jiro," I said. "Let's get together again."

"Sure," he said. "Let's."

I waited in the car to make sure Jiro's truck would start. It started easily and several times Jiro raced the motor. When the motor was finally warm Jiro waved his hand and the truck shot up the street and was gone.

—1941

# The Sweet Potato

It was the last day at Treasure Island and Hiro took me around for a last look. Time after time he shook his head as he fondly gazed at the buildings. The lights were going out at midnight.

"Gee, it gets me," he said, his eyes becoming red. "I don't like it."

All summer we had gone to the Fair together. There were days when I would rather have stayed at home, but Hiro would come and pull me out of the house.

"I'm sick. I want companionship. Please come with me and make me happy," he would beg.

Each time it ended the same way. We would walk for miles, and he would talk. We saw very little of the exhibits. When we became tired we would go up on the Temple Compound and rest. Each time we would look below and watch the crowd coming and going. And each time Hiro would comment, "Gee, look at those people going back and forth. Wandering forever . . . that's what we're all doing. Searching for something, searching for the real thing. . . . everyone of us. Look at them going in circles. That's us when we go below and join them."

I knew what was coming next. All summer we had argued about ourselves . . . the problem of the second generation of Japanese ancestry. "I tell you. We're not getting anywhere. We haven't a chance," he would tell me. "We'll fall into our parents' routine life and end there. We'll have our own clique and never get out of it."

"You're wrong, Hiro," I would say. "We'll climb and make ourselves heard. We have something in us to express and we will be heard."

107

Hiro would shake his head. "You write stories and sing in the clouds. You dream too much."

Over and over we would talk and disagree. Whenever the situation became unpleasant we would become silent and walk. After a time the holiday spirit of the Island would take hold of us and we would become lively again.

"It's this friendly spirit around here I like," I would tell him. "I hope it never fades."

"Same here," he would agree. "But the Fair will be over and there'll be no more. Let's go and see the Cavalcade once more."

On the last day at the Fair we walked much and said little. Our legs were aching but we did not rest. Hiro was almost crying. "Here's this wonderful thing called the Fair ending tonight, definitely at midnight. The place where people came to forget awhile and laugh and sing. Tomorrow the Island will be empty and dark." I said nothing.

"What do you think?" he asked me suddenly. "Do you think our people will ever be noticed favorably? What can we Japanese do? Must we accomplish big things here in America?"

"Little things can accomplish big things too. I think," I said.

"That's right," he agreed. "But it's so slow. It takes time."

At three in the afternoon we became hungry. All the eating places were filled and we had to hunt around for a place to eat. "Let's go to the Japanese Tearoom today," Hiro suggested. "We might find a table there." I agreed.

The place was filled and we had to wait for a table but we finally got one. All about us were the white people munching teacakes, sipping Japan tea, and tasting green tea ice cream. Hiro's face reddened a bit. Long secluded in the Japanese community, he looked shy and awkward. But it did not last long.

An old white lady and a young man came over to the table and asked if we would share the table with them. We readily consented. Suddenly, the old lady began to speak in Japanese.

"How are you?" she said. "Isn't it a wonderful afternoon?"

"You speak Japanese," I said, amazed.

"A little," she explained in Japanese. "I was in Japan for several years. I was in Yokohama during the big earthquake."

The young man spoke in English. "My mother and I love Japan. Have you ever been there?"

Hiro and I shook our heads. "No. We'd like to some day."

"You should visit Japan. It's a beautiful country," the young man said.

The old lady continued in Japanese. "I taught in the grade school for five years. When the earthquake came we lost everything. Fortunately my family came out alive."

"I was small then," the son said. "One day the houses were all standing in Yokohama and the next day there was nothing. It happened very quickly."

"It must've been terrible," Hiro said. "I guess there was food shortage."

"Yes, there was food shortage." The old lady nodded her head. "There wasn't enough food to go around. Do you know? There was one experience I'll always remember."

"She likes to tell it to everybody," the son said, smiling. "I remember."

"We were without food on the first day," she continued. "Nobody had food. A Japanese family whom we did not know, found a single sweet potato. There were four in their family but the father cut the potato in eight parts and gave each of us a cube. The four in our family were never more filled. I cannot forget it. And afterwards a boy came along with a cupful of sterilized water and we shared that too."

"That potato was really sweet," the son said.

We nodded and said nothing. Hiro's eyes twinkled, looking first at the old lady and her son and then me. "Where do you live now?" he asked the young man.

"In Sacramento," replied the young man. "We come to San Francisco often. And whenever we do we feast on Japanese food."

"I like daikon, miso, tofu, tempura, and things cooked with shoyu," the old lady said.

"And mochi," added the young man. The old lady laughed. "My boy likes rice cake best."

"Do you like raw fish?" I asked them.

"Very much, with mustard and shoyu," was the young man's reply. "There's one thing I don't go for."

"That's the octopus," the old lady said. "It's like rubber and there's no taste."

"Say, what's going to happen to the Japanese Pavilion?" The young man suddenly changed the subject. I said it probably would be torn down.

"That's a shame." He shook his head sadly. "A beautiful building like this."

"This is a beautiful day," said the old lady. "Warm and serene. A beautiful setting for the last day."

"It certainly is," I agreed.

Hiro beamed and looked gaily about, forgetting time and place. The four of us sat there a long time as if we had known one another a good many years. The people looked curiously at us, wondering what we had in common.

—1941

# Strange Bedfellows

AT THE HOME of Tanaka three odd characters met one evening—odd because in the company of three they were strange bedfellows. Fate allowing, the two Nisei converged upon the Issei, Tanaka, at an identical time. In the company of the third member, they had never been together before. Now the two Nisei blinked their eyes and nodded their heads as the host introduced them.

Tom looked questioningly at Tanaka. His eyes became doubtful. He sideglanced at the other Nisei, Tetsuo, as if his presence were unwanted. Evidently he did not like him.

"Well, what is it, Tom?" asked Tanaka, puffing at his pipe and looking contentedly at his company. He noticed the uneasy air but remained unruffled.

"Nothing," was Tom's reply.

Tanaka smiled. "Oh yes, you have. You can't hide your tell-tale face."

Tom did not answer right away. He evaded the Issei's eyes.

"What brought you here tonight, Tom?" patiently asked Tanaka.

"I came to tell you about something," Tom admitted finally.

"Oh," The old man's eyes lit up. It gave him great pleasure when young men sought him out. He liked young people for their vast possibilities in life. And in turn, he disliked them for whatever limited roles they assigned themselves to, sacrificing their potentialities.

Nisei approached him out of their curiosity. They derided him behind his back. They called him "the local puzzle." But always they returned to try their wits against the old man who had never been

**111**

argued down. So Tanaka understood the purpose of the young men's visit.

He waved his hand assuringly. "Go right ahead, Tom. If I know you, you are going to say something which will be very interesting to Tetsuo. Yes, he will be very much concerned."

Tetsuo gazed doubtfully at his old friend. Tanaka could not be serious. He had heard of Tom's reputation as an atheist. Why, it was absurd.

Tanaka looked at his charges and chuckled inwardly. A community leader like Tetsuo looked him up. A college graduate like Tom debated with him. And at one time he was illiterate. Back in Japan he had dropped out of the elementary in his third year. He came to America and learned how to sign his name, but that was all. In the space of time, he learned how to read Japanese papers. He read books, listened to others and lived.

"I came to tell you that you're all wrong," Tom said to Tanaka. "After thinking it over I'm convinced that I'm right."

"Yes?" Tanaka smiled and continued puffing at his pipe. "No, you're wrong, Tom. It may be true for others but not for you."

Tom waved his hand in protest. "Come now, Tanaka. Don't get me worked up just for argument's sake. Once is enough. Say you agree with me."

"When you say it, Tom, it becomes wrong. For some others it may be true."

"There's no God," cried Tom heatedly. "Science has proved this many times!"

"To you there is God."

Tom laughed outright. "Don't make me laugh. If there is God why hasn't he saved mankind. Don't tell me that all of us who are involved in this great war are beasts and deserve suffering. Surely, some are innocent, and why are they being punished?"

"There is God," cut in Tetsuo, unable to hold himself back any longer. "Tanaka is right. You cannot deny His existence."

"All right," said Tom, turning to Tetsuo. "Prove it."

"God made us so . . ." began Tetsuo.

Tanaka held up his hand to Tetsuo, and the latter paused. "Tom, don't think in general terms," Tanaka said slowly. "Lay off the society ills and sufferings. That doesn't concern you at this time. Don't think society represents you nor don't think God is looking for you. Forget them. Come down to yourself—probe yourself. You must find yourself within your realm—not anywhere else. Forget the world."

"Yes, there is God," Tetsuo emphatically chimed in. "God is over us and . . . ."

Tanaka hushed him. Now he turned his attention to the young people's church leader. "To you there is no God."

For a moment the young man stood speechless. He looked at Tanaka for a hint of spoofing, but the old man was all seriousness. "I believe in God; I work for . . . ." he protested.

"I still say there is no God."

Tetsuo appeared bewildered. First he looked at the old man and then Tom. "A minute ago you told him . . . ."

"That was for Tom—not you," asserted Tanaka. Forget what you learned. You missed the boat. Start all over again. You don't know your ABC."

Tanaka knocked his pipe against the side of his shoe and rose to his feet. It was his signal for the end of the evening's session.

Outside Tom and Tetsuo walked alongside of each other.

"Isn't Tanaka a case?" exclaimed Tetsuo. "All he thinks about is winning arguments."

Tom laughed. "He's a crackpot."

"My evening was wasted listening to him."

"Never again," agreed Tom.

They reached the crossroad, and the pair paused awhile.

"Certainly, there's God," Tetsuo stated as if to clarify himself.

"Aw, don't give me that crap," Tom said disgustedly. "There's no God."

—1949

# VI
# THE WAR YEARS

# 1, 2, 3, 4,
# Who Are We For?

IN CHINATOWN THESE two shops stand side by side. It is late in the afternoon and the people on their way home stop to make purchases. Finally the last minute rush is over. The streets become empty, the shops become quiet. The clerks of the two places rest. The driver for Nippon Company comes out to the truck to haul in vegetables and fruits. A clerk in a canvas apron appears in the doorway of the other shop.

"Hi, Jimmy," called the Nippon Company driver.

"Hello, Harry," said Jimmy Chang of Chang and Sons Company. "Been pretty busy a few minutes ago, eh?"

"You bet," Harry said. He grins but doesn't stop loading his baskets with the greens and fruits. He works for the boss.

"How's business on the route?" Jimmy asked.

"Slow," said Harry Sasayama. "Plenty slow. Think business will pick up this year?"

"I don't know. I really don't know," said Jimmy. He stands idly by the doorway. Jimmy Chang is one of the sons of Papa Chang.

Harry goes in with a load. When he comes out to the street again Jimmy Chang is still standing on the same spot.

"Who's going to win the American League this year?" he called out to Harry.

"The Yanks. They're cinch."

Jimmy laughs. They both like the Yankees, Joe DiMaggio, Gehrig, Dickey and Company.

"Who's going to win the National?"

"Chicago Cubs."

Jimmy's grin grows wider. "You're wrong there, Harry," he said. "I like the Giants. I bet it'll be another nickel world series."

"No sir," Harry said. "Not this year. It's not in the cards."

Jimmy is grinning. "I still like the Giants," he said.

Jimmy Chang comes out to the truck and lends a hand. He picks up cabbages, lettuces, and cauliflowers and fills the baskets. "You like the Cubs the way you like Max Baer against Joe Louis," he said.

"Let me tell you something, Jimmy," said Harry. "Don't sell Max Baer short, I'm not kidding."

Harry Sasayama lifts the baskets and goes in the shop. Jimmy leans against the truck and watches a few strollers go by. Harry is back. Jimmy is ready with the oranges this time.

"Do you know who I saw this afternoon?" he said.

"No. Who?" said Harry.

"A beautiful Japanese girl," Jimmy said.

Harry laughs. "That's a fine way to tell a friend," he said.

"I think you know her, Yoshiko Saito," said Jimmy.

Harry keeps his lips closed. After a while he talks. "Chinese girls are prettier," he said. "I don't know why but they're prettier than the Japanese girls."

"So you've quarreled again," Jimmy said.

"Ask any Japanese fellows and they'll tell you Chinese girls are prettier."

"Now I know you're not speaking to her," Jimmy said.

"You mean she's not speaking to me," Harry said.

Jimmy Chang grins. "All right. She's not speaking to you. She spoke to me though."

"That doesn't interest me," Harry said.

"She said she's going to the dance at the Fairmont next Saturday," Jimmy informed.

"It's all right with me," Harry said.

"A city fellow's taking her," Jimmy said.

"It's still all right with me," Harry said.

They finish filling the baskets. They stop. The clock says it's six-thirty. In a few minutes Harry is through with work.

"I don't see you at the Lakeside Courts anymore. Don't you play tennis there?" Jimmy asked.

"No," said Harry. "I've laid off tennis."

"We miss you at Lakeside," said Jimmy. "She still comes there."

Harry Sasayama shrugs his shoulders.

"What do you say we go out there together next Sunday? We'll meet her," said Jimmy.

"I tell you I quit tennis," Harry told him.

Jimmy scratches his head. "How in the hell did you two fall in love with each other?"

The boss calls Harry from the store. Harry swings his baskets up and goes inside. When he comes out Jimmy Chang is waiting for him.

"Where are you going, Harry?" said Jimmy.

"I'm driving the truck in the garage. Jump in."

Jimmy gets in. "About Yoshiko Saito . . ." he began.

"Cut it out will you?" Harry said. "Stop mentioning her. Talk about something else."

'All right," Jimmy Chang said brightly. "Let's take today's headlines. War Crisis in Europe. U.S. Pleas for Peace."

"That's another subject I worry about. I hate war. All I want is peace in the world," said Harry.

"I hope there's no world war again," said Jimmy. "If we have another one we'll all lose. Everybody."

"There'll be another one pretty soon," Harry said.

"Do you think so, Harry?"

"There'll be another big one pretty soon," Harry said.

"What does a war do for the people?" What do we get out of it?" Jimmy said. "Look at the war in China. War is a bigger machine than people. Once it starts it'll crush the people."

"War is terrible," Harry Sasayama said.

"It's horrible," said Jimmy.

"Lucky we're in America," said Harry. "If you were in China and I was in Japan we'd be taking shots at each other."

Harry starts the truck. They drive around the block and reach the garage. Harry locks the place. They walk back.

"Misunderstanding—misunderstanding causes war," said Harry. "There's misunderstanding on both sides."

"Do you believe our strength and weakness in nature produce war?" asked Jimmy.

"Yes," said Harry.

They walk slowly. They stop in front of the cigar stand. "Let's get a Coca Cola," Harry said. "I'm thirsty."

"No, thanks," said Jimmy. "I drank too much beer this afternoon."

Harry walks on.

"What's the matter? I thought you were thirsty," said Jimmy.

"I'll wait till you get thirsty," said Harry.

Jimmy laughs. "If you get along with Yoshiko Saito as we do together you'd be married to her."

Harry looks as if he did not hear Jimmy. "When war comes to a country the people have no choice. They go to war or get court-martialed."

"Right," agreed Jimmy. "They fight with belief or they go with duty."

"If America goes to war where would you stand?" Harry asked Jimmy.

"That depends on the people," Jimmy said. "If the people decide a war is the only solution I'll go."

"I want to tell you a story I heard," Harry said. "A new teacher filled in as a substitute in one of the grammar schools. She saw one small Oriental boy walking by in the school yard. She couldn't tell whether he was Chinese or Japanese. She was curious. So she stopped him. 'Are you Japanese or Chinese?' she asked the small boy. The little boy looked at the new teacher and sort of sniffed the air. Then he straightened himself, pushed out his chest, and said, 'I'm an American.'"

Jimmy Chang grins broadly. "So the new teacher never found out his nationality," he said. "What was he?"

Harry grins. "I don't know."

"That's America. We don't know," Jimmy said.

They reach Jimmy Chang's store. They stop by the front and look in. "Nothing doing tonight," Jimmy said.

"I must be going," Harry said.

"Where are you going tonight," asked Jimmy.

"No place," said Harry.

"You should do something about Yoshiko Saito," said Jimmy.

"You worry more about her than I do," said Harry.

Jimmy nods his head. "I hate to see a ripe apple hanging ready to fall."

"What do you mean by that," asked Harry.

"Forget it," said Jimmy. "Say. Hedy Lamarr's picture is in town."

"I know. She's at Roxie," Harry said.

"Let's take it in tomorrow night," said Jimmy. "Forget Loretta Young for one night."

"Loretta Young is beautiful," Harry said.

"You and Loretta Young," Jimmy said.

Harry Sasayama starts moving away.

"Hey. Tomorrow night . . . is it a go?" asked Jimmy.

Harry nods.

"Look out," cried Jimmy. "Catch it."

Harry catches two apples thrown by Jimmy Chang.

"See you in the morning," Jimmy said.

Harry waves his hand with a half-eaten apple and walks down the street.

—1940

# The Long Journey
# and the Short Ride

THE OTHER DAY my brother and I got to talking of the World War II days. It seemed so long ago, we agreed. The mild California climate of San Leandro was much to our liking, inasmuch being our hometown. We were back home again.

My brother looked pensively out into the yard and beyond the near-by hills as if he were re-living the past, momentarily forgetting his helpless legs and wheelchair living.

"Do you remember the last leave you got before you went overseas?" I said.

His eyes kept staring eastward over the hills but I knew he had heard me. Once again I saw him in his khaki uniform—young and healthy sergeant of the 442nd Infantry Regiment. Again I saw Mom alive and excited as ever as she saw in flesh her youngest son. She had not seen him in two years—she as an enemy alien in the Utah detention camp and her son in the army cap. Ironic? But it was so. A few Nisei in the camp would ask why in the sam hill had he chosen to spend his leave in a dump like Topaz War Relocation Center— why not the bright lights and the free "outside" world?

"I came to spend a few days with my family," he would say. Then others would ask why he remained in the army. "Because I trust the government of my country," he would say.

Our mother and father were living then. We had been a tight little family group. As my brother's eyes dreamily stared into the past, I could imagine how much he had missed the family life during the war

years and since then, not counting what he had gone through at the
front.

"Do you remember the time Mom and I saw you off on your last
leave?" I said.

My brother nodded his head and smiled. "Sure do," he said.

How many times he had heard the story I have forgotten, but I am
continually retelling it because of its lasting impression on me—of my
country and the little people representing it in time of war and
turmoil.

At the gatehouse in front of the administration building we stood
in line waiting for our names to be checked off the passenger list.
Mother and I were accompanying my brother to Delta station to see
him off for the last time.

It was a rare occasion for us to leave the camp and go "outside" to
the town. We had to have a special permit with a reasonable and
specific purpose.

As we passed the gate and boarded the bus to Delta an internal
security clerk counted the heads for a final check-up. Finally we were
on our way. At our first glance back, we saw nothing but the fence
enclosure. Gradually our perspective restored, we saw our hospital
building and water tank. Now the Military Police barracks were becoming blurred and a speck in the distance. Mother and I were "outside" for the first time.

We faced the future with misgivings and apprehension—especially
the immediate present. What will it be like to be on the "outside?"
For being cooped up as we were, perhaps, our imagination played
tricks. We had been away for so long from the normal atmosphere.

About midway to the town of Delta the bus slowed down. Up ahead
stood the MP gatehouse. A soldier climbed aboard to check the passenger list. He tallied the number of names on his paper and the number of heads on the bus. Having satisfied himself, the MP jumped off
and waved the bus away.

To my brother it must have been all a puzzle. In the first place, he
must have asked himself, what we were doing out in the middle of the
Utah desert. Fortunately for me, he never did ask me why—why his
family had been evacuated from their home on the West Coast.

From my standpoint as a camp resident, I had a different puzzle.
How will a camp resident be received on the "outside?"

The train was on time. Once at the station there was little time for
brooding. I shook hands with my brother. Mother took him aside for
the last few precious minutes. She said, "Be careful, my boy. Take
good care of yourself."

"Don't worry, Mom. I'll be back," my brother said.

The station platform was quite filled with groups of white folks. In my concern for my brother and mother, I had not noticed anything unusual—incidents unpleasant or otherwise.

It was long after the train whistle had died down that I observed the bleak loneliness of the station. A moment ago a train-load of people with a purpose of duty was here and now I must go back to my camp, I thought. As I guided my mother down the dirt road toward the town, the vast emptiness of the desert sunset depressed me. A fitting description for my "inside" life, I thought.

Walking with my head down and watching our feet raise puffs of dust in the air, I had not at first noticed the car stopping alongside of us nor the voice calling us. A friendly middle-aged couple and their teenage daughter were smiling at us. "Going back to town? Hop in," the white man said. At the same time the girl in the rear seat opened the door for us.

The swift change of climate dumbfounded me. All the way to town, which was only a few blocks away from the station, we exchanged family news with the white folks. They had just seen their boy off after a short shore leave. They had noticed Mother and I with my brother at the station. For all the good their friendly gesture had done for me, all I could say in words was a simple thanks. It was a short ride, sure enough, but the most memorable, coming at the right moment for us—especially for me.

Home again together after going our separate ways, we made the most of it. Many days along with many events had gone by since then. My brother who had fought almost a year in France and Italy was wounded in the last Italian campaign of the war. Then a series of hospital transfers finally ended at the Letterman in San Francisco. Our mother and father and I returned from camp to California when the war with Japan was reaching near the climax. Mother and I made numerous visits to see my brother at the DeWitt Hospital in Auburn, California and the Letterman before she died. She never saw him discharged for home. Then Father passed on.

Today the spring sun is shining bright in San Leandro. From the kitchen in his new home my brother and I gazed at the familiar surroundings now interspersed with the town's growth. He had built his new home under the disabled veteran's benefit. It was his pride and joy. "You're doing all right," I said.

My brother nodded and said, "Thought I'd never make it. It sure was a long journey home—for both of us."

Mother always used to worry about getting my brother married

early and settled down, even during the war years. After he had returned home totally paralyzed and had to live on a wheelchair I too
was worried. I was afraid that he would never find a wife. After he
had completed furnishing his new house I used to egg him on, if only
to encourage him. "Now all you need is a bride."

Today he is married. He had found his life partner just about a year
ago.

"Mom got the roughest part of the deal," I said "She never saw you
recover."

There was a tinge of sorrow in my brother's voice. Not with bitterness and despair but with calm and contentment, he said, "If only
she could see me now."

—1959

# The Travelers

AT THE GATEHOUSE in front of the administration building stood the travelers, waiting for their names to be checked off the passenger list. Along the fence were lined their friends and well-wishers. The day was fine for a last farewell at the gate as the crowd of several hundred persons would assure. Here and there the Internal Security workers darted as last-minute communications occupied their attention. A truck bearing the baggage of relocatees slowly cut a path into the crowd and stopped beyond the fence. The travelers' eyes anxiously peered into the canvas-covered truck for a reassuring glance at their belongings. The load was a good one for there were nine persons, including a child, heading for all points east.

At last the overdue bus for the town of Delta appeared on the scene. A flurry of cries and gestures sent off the nine as the group boarded the bus. Now the shoppers to Delta milled about the gate for the choice seats remaining in the car. Their grinning and nonchalant faces, as they walked beyond the gate to the car, bore the jibes of their acquaintances who reminded them not to get lost in town and to be sure and return to Topaz.

For a final check-up a clerk boarded the bus and counted the heads, and the driver, racing the motor, impatiently watched for the "go" signal. As the bus pulled away from the gatehouse, the passengers frantically looked back and waved to the people along the fence. The car picked up speed and the folks settled back in their seats. Now the hospital was passed; the water tank and the MP barracks became blurred and a speck in the distance.

A small child who was clinging to her mother's hand stood in her seat with her nose flat against the window. "Look, Mommy. Our camp looks like a toyhouse now," she cried.

The mother gazed over her shoulder and nodded her head. "Yes, Mary. In a few minutes we shall see no more of it. Topaz will become a memory."

The little girl began to sob as she settled down in her seat. "I'm going to miss Sachi and Dorothy and Miye . . ."

"Hush, child," soothed the Issei woman. "You shall make many new friends. Do not cry."

After awhile the child dried her tears and blew her nose with a handkerchief, and presently her eyes followed the horizon, sweeping at a glance the autumn scene in the foreground. The corn stalks were turning brown; the harvested alfalfa fields looked bare and dry and the trees had shed their leaves.

Behind the little girl sat an aged woman who now leaned forward and patted the head of the child. "You're a very brave little girl," she said, smiling. As the child's mother glanced back, she addressed her, "Where are you heading for? You are courageous—an Issei very seldom relocates by herself."

The younger woman smiled and patted her girl's shoulder. "I am not alone—she's with me. We are going to Kansas City for her education. There I shall enter the domestic world again, and Mary shall go to school. I want so badly to give her the best education that I am willing to slave and scrimp the rest of my days."

The aged woman looked dubious but nodded sympathetically. She looked about the car with interest. She could easily tell apart the relocatees from the shoppers by the respective type of clothes they wore. Her ears caught the conversation of the shoppers' group.

"My husband wants me to get a pair of small hinges and a gallon of ivory paint. Also he told me to look around for electric sockets and plugs."

"Do you know what I'm going to do first? Buy clothes and groceries? No! I'm going to get me a couple of hamburgers and coffee at the restaurant, and then at Thornton's gorge myself on a chocolate nut sundae. That's what I'll do."

"I have a lot of birthday presents to buy for my children. Yes, three of the kids will be having their birthdays in the next four months. Have you been out to town lately? What have they in way of children's toys and clothes?"

The aged woman studied the travelers with growing curiosity. There was a young girl in a smart Chesterfield coat reading the train schedule, and across from her sat another Nisei girl, her face flushed and her eyes sparkling with adventure. Surely, a pair of relocatees, thought the old woman.

The bus began to slow down, and the eyes of the passengers looked ahead. In front of the MP gatehouse the car stopped and a soldier came aboard to check the passenger list. He tallied the number of names on the paper with the number of heads and jumped off, waving the bus away.

Once more the journey to Delta was resumed, and the folks settled back in their seats. The aged woman continued gazing at her fellow travelers. Once, twice, she smiled to herself. She noticed the solemnity and independence of the relocatees and the boisterousness and companionship of the shoppers' group. "On the way . . . our journey," she whispered softly to herself. "Travelers . . . we are all travelers on the earth."

In the middle of her thoughts, the woman sitting in front of her spoke to her. "May I ask where you are going? I don't suppose you are going shopping. You don't look it."

The old woman chuckled softly, and then grasping the sleeve of the young man sitting beside her said, "This is my boy and I am seeing him off. Roy is on his way to Camp Shelby."

For the first time the mother and her child noticed the youth in a private's uniform. Mary's eyes were quick to see that the soldier was a recent volunteer. His shoulder insignia was missing. The little girl became shy as the soldier's humor-filled eyes met hers.

Now the coach crossed the overpass and reached the downhill grade. The soldier's eyes followed the course of the Sevier River until the steep bank masked the scene.

"In a few minutes we'll be in Delta," a voice informed the crowd in general.

At last, thought the soldier. His eyes anxiously looked ahead but presently he turned to gaze on his mother. Their eyes met. "Don't worry about me, Mama. I'll be all right," he said.

The mother slowly nodded her head.

As the bus turned left at the crossroad, the eyes of the passengers were focused to the right on a big bird that floated indifferently in the air.

"How symmetrical and natural!" exclaimed someone in the group.

"Picture of an idyl," cried another. "How lucky the birds are. They can live in spite of a war-torn world."

"The people, too, will survive this war," quickly commented the soldier's mother from the rear.

In an instant the attention of the travelers was on the tiny old woman sitting beside the soldier. The girl whose sparkling eyes spoke adventure gazed respectfully at her, and smiling thus, her features effused silent applause. In a fraction of a second the soldier caught the lively eyes of the girl. A moment later their eyes met again. The town of Delta loomed ahead.

Beautiful, thought the soldier. What have I been doing all this time in Topaz? Who is she? Where is she going? Instinctively, he looked at his watch. Time was short. He gathered up his heavy army coat and duffle bag. The bus turned left into the dirt road that wound up at the station. In front of the baggage room the bus stopped to let off the train passengers and the soldier's mother.

The soldier and his mother stood in front of the station, watching the others enter the station to purchase their tickets. Soon a party of Caucasian travelers and their friends appeared from the waiting room. Among them were a sailor and a corporal, presumably returning to their duty.

"Let's go inside and see if the train is on time," suggested the boy to his mother.

Inside, the small waiting room was packed with Salt Lake-bound travelers. Roy and his mother stood near the center of the room where the unfired coal stove was located.

"The train is on time, Mama," he announced to her, looking at the bulletin board. "It's pulling in at 2:30."

The mother nodded her head. "Only thirty minutes more, Roy," she said.

A youth of eighteen or nineteen years of age approached the old woman, "There's a seat for you, *oba-san*. Take it because you'll have some time to wait yet."

The mother politely refused the first time but with repeated offerings, she thanked the Nisei and accepted the seat on the bench.

"Where are you going . . . to college?" asked the soldier to the hatless youth who offered the seat.

The latter agreed. "I'm going to the University of Wisconsin. That's in Madison, Wisconsin, you know."

"So you're going to Wisconsin, eh?" questioned a dapper Nisei in a well-tailored suit and topcoat. "Boy, we Nisei are certainly traveling nowadays. We're like the seeds in the wind. Now, I'm going to New York. I always wanted to see the big city but I was a tied-down man. Here I am now with an opportunity to start all over again."

"You look successful," commented the soldier. "What were you doing before the war?"

"I used to operate a drive-in market in the south . . . Los Angeles, I mean," replied the man. "I used to have a good business but had to sell the place for almost nothing. Oh well, that's past."

The soldier was curious. He asked the man what his purpose was in going to New York, but his eyes searched for the girl he saw in the bus. She was seated at the end of the bench talking with the girl who still held the train schedule in her gloved hand.

The dapper Nisei shrugged his shoulders. "I'm just going to New York on a hunch. I want to feel my way around before I settle down. By the time I call my wife and kids I want to be sitting pretty."

"You aren't thinking of going back to California?" asked the young student.

"No," he said emphatically. "To my way of thinking, California is a poor proposition for Nisei. Why should I wait several more years for an admission permit or stall around for the postwar period before staking myself in the outside world?"

A tall Nisei with powerful shoulders, who was leaning against the wall and talking to a baggage man, chucked his cigarette away and approached the group. "You folks travelin' too? he said pleasantly. "Anyone goin' my way . . . Akron, Ohio?"

The dapper Nisei chuckled softly. "It seems we have different choices. This fellow here is going to study in Madison, Wisconsin, and, of course, this soldier is going to Shelby, Mississippi. And I'm heading for New York. By the way, where is that Issei woman with the child going?"

"She's going to Missouri . . . Kansas City," said the soldier.

"And where you girls goin'?" asked the Nisei with hefty shoulders, turning to the two Nisei girls.

The soldier watched the girl with the sparkling eyes glance at the group before replying.

"I am going to Chicago . . . a job is waiting for me in the office of a big firm, and she," indicating her companion, "is getting married in Philadelphia."

Fascinating, thought the soldier. I'd like to know her better. Oh, why does life offer me things at the last moment?

The Nisei with the powerful shoulders shifted his weight from one foot to the other, grinning at the girls. "Chicago . . . Philadelphia . . . Kansas City . . . New York . . . Camp Shelby . . . Madison . . . Akron. Ain't it strange we meet here? One hour and we part once and for all. Maybe we'll never meet again, eh?"

"I'm going out to see if the train is in sight," the student announced, going to the door.

The girl, who was bound for a Chicago office, giggled excitedly and her voice trembled a little. "This is my first trip away from the folks.

Oh, I'm so thrilled. Ever since graduating from high school I've been a domestic worker, and now I am going to be a stenographer . . . a white collar job. Isn't it exciting?"

"I'm a farmer from Northern California," said the Nisei with the big shoulders. "My friend calls me from Ohio. He says there's plenty of farms . . . many 100-acre farms for sale at reasonable prices. Can you image? For $2000 to $4000 you can buy such farms with farm-houses and buildings. Yeah, even a lot costs $2000 back in California."

The soldier's mother beckoned her son, and the latter walked over to the bench. "Isn't it about time for the train to arrive, Roy?" she asked anxiously.

"It ought to be here in five minutes, Mama," said her son. He helped his mother to her feet.

"Let us wait outside," the mother said.

The Chicago-bound girl smiled at him, and he hesitated in his steps. For a second his mind raced with frenzied thoughts: Hello, lovely. Let's get acquainted; let's travel through life together for awhile. Okay?

Then suddenly, resolutely, the soldier lifted his head high and turned on his heels, heading for the door. The young student ran in excitedly, "The train . . . it's coming, folks."

Outside, the group watched the distant speck on the horizon grow-ing ever larger. Soon the virgin Utah sky of the moment was darkened with black smoke. The Challenger had reached Delta on time.

The little group rushed forward, their companionship of a moment ago forgotten, and they sought seats in several cars. Only the soldier and his mother stalled for time. "Don't worry about me, Mama. I'll be all right so take good care of yourself," he said.

The mother waved her hand as the train slowly began to move.

Once on the train the clan dispersed. Soldiers, bright and friendly, were everywhere. And the Japanese faces were now lost in the crowd as they should be.

As the soldier's mother slowly trudged along the dirt road toward Delta, a car stopped alongside her. A Caucasian and his wife were signaling her to get into the car. From the rear of the sedan a girl opened the door for her. For a moment, she hesitated and then said, "Thank you."

"Come in. We'll give you a ride to town," the girl said, smiling.

The aged woman climbed aboard with the help of the girl. All the way to town, which was only a few blocks away from the station, the group did not chat for they had no common language, but understood the trials and errors of a traveler's way.

—1943

# The Man with
# Bulging Pockets

THERE WAS A man at Tanforan Assembly Center who was noted for his bulging pockets and for his admiring following. From the first day he stepped into the grounds of the former racetrack he was singled out by the young, and not many days passed when everyone began to call him "Grandpa." That was the beginning of his growing fame, perhaps unequaled by anyone at Tanforan with the exception of the most noted thoroughbreds of the prewar days. His smiling old face, wrinkled with time and energy, bobbed in and out of the children's gathering. Whenever he went the cries of "Grandpa! Here comes Grandpa!" trailed him, and his smile broadened more than ever.

No one in the community ever saw him before and for a long while people did not know where he lived. Then one day his young friends trailed him to his room which he shared with his wife. Day after day the chilren came to his door, calling his name, and when home he would open his door and come out with a boxful of candies. Children with sharp eyes began to notice his specially made pockets all over his coat and they would cluster around him with wide-open eyes for surprise and sweets.

As the people from many communities of the Bay Region entered the gates of the center they soon learned of Grandpa, the man with a houseful of candies and sweets, and his unaccountable amount of cash in the bank. Some of his new acquaintances swore that he was the richest man in Tanforan with hidden treasure in every state of the union while others claimed that he had retired with several thousand

in cash and was using it as "candy money" for the children. When the
old folks commended him for his generosity he simply smiled and
brushed off the compliment but when someone in his young following
asked him how rich he was, he would give some kind of an answer.

"Yes, Sammy," he would say and nod. "I am rich. I am not rich
with money perhaps but I am rich. I am rich for I think I am rich, and
I have no aim for money-making now."

But Sammy was still curious. "But if you were poor would you like
to be rich with money so you could buy us candy?"

Grandpa would then slap his knees and roar with laughter and nod
his head. "Yes, Sammy. Then I would like to be rich with money."

As the number of his friends grew Grandpa found himself short of
help and soon the spry Sammy was appointed the head assistant. On
Grandpa's daily walk around the center Sammy would accompany
him and assist in passing out the sweets. From all barracks the boys
and girls would come running with shouts of glee, dropping their toys
and playthings. Boys in high spirits would confide in him their hope
and ambitions, making Grandpa smile.

"When I grow big I'll buy tobacco for Grandpa. I'll buy many cans
of the best for him," one of the boys would cry.

"Grandpa, we'll all buy tobaccos for you. So many tobaccos that
you won't ever have to worry about it," the second boy would exclaim.

"Yes?" Grandpa would ask with a twinkle in his eyes.

"You bet your life," a chorus would reply.

"Thank you, thank you," Grandpa would say and pat the uplifted
heads.

"And when you die, Grandpa, we'll carry your coffin to the grave.
We'll remember you, Grandpa. Always," Sammy would exclaim.

Grandpa would chuckle and nod his head in appreciation. "Now I
feel safe and comfortable no matter what happens. But if you wish to
carry my coffin, you boys must eat and sleep a lot and grow big and
strong."

As the center grew in population all sorts of people began to crop
out and even Grandpa had his troubles. Out of the thousands of newcomers who had come later an old bachelor who was once a friend
of Grandpa's looked enviously at his popularity. The children called
him The Old Man. With shrewd eyes he took to the trails of Grandpa's
daily round, seeking a bigger following than Grandpa's and a greater
popularity. He soon learned that Grandpa's daily work began at eight
in the morning from the west end of the center, so The Old Man set
his walking hour half an hour later to undo whatever Grandpa had
accomplished for the day.

For a short while Grandpa did not know he had a rival until one day one of his young friends told him about an old man who also came around with candies and sweets.

"Fine, fine! He must be a very nice man," Grandpa heartily cried. "Don't you find his candies good too?"

"Yes, he gives us more than you, Grandpa," one of the boys said.

"Is that so? He must be rich then, both in money and otherwise," Grandpa said.

"I do not like him, Grandpa. He gives us lots of candies but still I do not like him," Sammy said.

Grandpa hushed Sammy so the other children would not hear. "Do not be too hasty, child. He must be nice to be so generous. You must give him time. Try and understand him."

"I still don't like him," Sammy replied.

The Old Man made very little progress with Grandpa's following but he began to look for the children of the newcomers and here he had luck. As time went on his following too became quite large but he was dissatisfied. He wanted Grandpa's following. He wished to be the only popular man of the center and this he earnestly set out to accomplish once and for all.

Grandpa's staunch young followers pleaded with Grandpa about the coming nemesis but he laughed it off.

"He's doing good, boys. He makes people happy. You should not tear down the good he is doing," Grandpa said.

"But he talks bad about you," his young friends cried.

Grandpa would not listen. "That is all talk, children. I would not believe such things until I hear directly from him."

At first Grandpa did not hear The Old Man talk, but one afternoon when he and Sammy were late going on their round he overheard the Old Man's words. The Old Man was talking to the young people.

"Grandpa is a no-good man. Do not accept his candy, boys and girls," the Old Man was saying. "His candies are bad and you mustn't touch them. Take mine."

Sammy pulled at Grandpa's sleeve. "Did you hear that, Grandpa? Did you hear The Old Man?"

Grandpa nodded his head quietly and continued walking. For a moment his face became stern and set, and his eyes were glued to the ground. Sammy watched him with concern.

"Don't feel bad, Grandpa. It's all right. We all like you," Sammy cried.

Grandpa patted his head and his familiar smile returned. Several minutes later he was roaring with laughter as he watched the youngsters romp around the playground. His eyes twinkled and his greetings reached the barracks where the children lived and played. His bulging pockets were reached into many times and soon they were emptied, and the youngsters sat around Grandpa munching their sweets and waiting for Grandpa's little stories. Grandpa looked at the gathering and beamed with pleasure. He watched the youngsters' faces whose features were yet unscarred by the wear and tear of life and nodded his head hopefully. He patted their heads and playfully pinched their cheeks. The youngsters noticed his silence and curiously looked at his face.

"What's the matter, Grandpa? What's wrong?" one tiny voice asked.

"Nothing, nothing. Everything is all right. Where the children live there is life. Do you know that, boys and girls? You are very valuable people. We old folks are worthless and some day you are going to take our places," said Grandpa.

The children jumped around happily. Their cries filled the air, and the passerbys beamed at the group. Grandpa waved his hands and began his story-telling. The youngsters leaned forward attentively. Suddenly the attention of the group was dispersed by whispers. The Old Man was coming up the road.

Grandpa hailed The Old Man but the latter walked by silently. He had two handfuls of candies, smiling at the children. Several of the youngsters ran after him, following him as he showered them with packages of gum and chocolate bars. The rest of the children watched hesitantly and then they saw Sammy sit down and lean closer to Grandpa to hear the story. The children followed suit and Grandpa looked at his crowd happily and smiled. He chuckled loudly and his little friends joined him.

"What is so funny, Grandpa?" Sammy asked innocently. "Aren't you mad at The Old Man?"

Grandpa shook his head and smiled. "I am not mad because I have many nice friends too. He needs nice little friends too, don't you think?"

The group remained silent, and Grandpa picked up his story. As he watched the rapt features of his little friends his face became lined with concern. In that moment of a dark recess a foreboding thought flashed in his mind. The Old Man and he belonged to one big circle where no ill feelings and furtive deeds need enter. They should join hands and rejoice in the heart of a child. They should inspire and sing in the oneness of hope, but no. They were partisans, and the split in their circle was the enigma and blot of all mankind.

—1944

# Unfinished Message

IT WAS ON a chilly May night in 1945 in the middle of Utah desert when my mother sharply called me. "I can't sleep tonight," she said. True, she had been fretting the past few nights, and I knew she was worried over her son at the Italian front.

I reassured her that everything would be all right. Hadn't he, I reasoned with her, come through without a scratch with a full year's service at the front, even with the 442nd Infantry Reiment?

"But I keep seeing Kazuo's face tonight," she said. "Each time I'm about to fall asleep his face keeps coming back."

I tried to calm her fears as best as I could. Nevertheless, she did not sleep that night.

The next night and the night following she slept fitfully more or less. Beneath her outward calm, however, she was under an ordeal only a mother could understand. "No news is good news. He's all right," I assured her.

A few days later we received a wire from the War Department that Kazuo had been seriously wounded. The news almost killed her. In the full medical report following we learned that he had a fractured skull but was resting peacefully. What struck me as odd was the day my brother was wounded. It was on May 5, the very night my mother was unable to sleep.

When we received word again, it was more cheerful. Kazuo was coming back on the hospital ship destined for home, and we were to decide the hospital nearest our home. We were still living in Topaz, Utah Relocation Center at the time, and the nearest available army hospital was the Fitzsimmons in Colorado.

"Let's have him transferred there so we can visit him as soon as he comes home," I said to Mother.

My mother would have none of it. "Do you think this is our real home? Our home is back in San Leandro, California. We'll be moving from here again, and Kazuo too will have to transfer. No, we'll go back and Kazuo can go to a hospital in California."

My mother couldn't get out of the camp soon enough. She counted the days when the next train to California would take us back home. In the meantime we learned that Kazuo was being transferred to DeWitt Army Hospital in Auburn, California.

On our trip home, our train stopped for a few minutes at Auburn, and our first urge was to get off the train and visit Kazuo. My mother stared toward the Auburn interiors. "It must be only a few miles from here. Here we are, so close to him and yet so far."

We heeded our good judgment and did not get off the train. "We must make ready our home. It must be in a mess. We must first go home and get busy cleaning the place. Our home must resemble our old home for Kazuo."

It took us two weeks to clean the house and settle down. My mother had to apply to the United States Attorney's office for a travel permit because she was an enemy alien and Japan and United States were still at war. Secure with a permit my mother accompanied me to Auburn. All the way on the bus to the hospital she nervously weighed the seriousness of Kazuo's actual condition. Are his legs all intact, are his hands there? she wondered. Can he see, is he normal mentally? It wasn't until she saw him in person did she feel relieved. He could see, his hands were useable, but his legs? Mother talked constantly on everything she could think of but his condition. Before long, she became aware of his actual condition.

In order to relieve ourselves of the hot valley air caught inside of the ward, my brother suggested sitting on the screened porch. It was when the ward boy saw my brother moving on the bed that he came to help him to his wheelchair. The ward boy bodily lifted him on the chair, and Mother saw my brother's spindly legs. He was unable to walk.

Afterwards, Mother asked me to inquire the doctor about Kazuo's condition. Will he ever walk? The doctor I talked to was not too hopeful, but I did not tell Mother.

"He says there's a fifty-fifty possibility that Kazuo will walk," I said to Mother.

Coming home, Mother said, "I'm worried over him. If I only could live long enough to see him fully recovered."

After another operation on his head, my brother was transfered to

Letterman Hospital in San Francisco, making possible weekly visits for Mother and I. Each time we saw him, she would take me aside and ask, "Do you think he's much improved? Isn't he better?"

That Christmas my brother got a two week furlough and came home for the first time since the war had started. I had to help him with his bath and toilet. My brother was confined to his wheelchair.

Time and again, Mother would ask me, "Will he ever walk again? I can't tell him that I worry over him."

Before my brother was released from the hospital, Mother died in her sleep on August 5, 1946. Although she complained of pains in the neck, we were totally unprepared for her death. Her doctor had previously diagnosed her symptoms as arthritis, but her death was sudden.

After her death our house became dark and silent. Even when my brother returned home for good in a wheelchair, the atmosphere was unchanged. We seemed to be companions in the dark. However, it changed one day.

As I sat quietly in the living room I heard a slight tapping on the window just above the divan where my mother had slept her last. When the taps repeated again, I went outside to check, knowing well that a stiff wind could move a branch of our lemon tree with a lemon or two tapping the wall of our house. There was no wind, no lemon near enough to reach the window. I was puzzled but did not confide in my brother when he joined me in the living room.

I had all but forgotten the incident when my brother and I were quietly sitting in the living room near the spot where our mother had passed away. For a while I was not conscious of the slight tapping on the window. When the repeated taps were loud enough to be heard clearly, I first looked at the window and then glanced at my brother. He too had heard the taps.

"Did you hear that?" I said.

My brother nodded. "Sure," he said. "Did you hear it too? I heard it the other day but I thought it was strange."

We looked at the window. There were no birds in sight, no lemons tapping. Then the taps repeated. After a few moments of silence I was about to comment when we heard the tapping again. This time I looked silently at my brother and on tiptoes approached the window. The tapping continued so I softly touched the window pane. The instant my fingers touched the glass, it stopped.

My brother and I looked at each other, silently aware that it must have been Mother calling our attention. At that instant I became conscious of the purpose of the mysterious taps. I couldn't help but recall Mother's words, "I can't stop worrying over you, my son."

The tappings stopped once and for all after that. We never heard it again after the message had reached us.

—1947

## Epilogue

This story was written nearly thirty years ago. My brother is alive and well, raising a family in San Leandro, California. He is still paralyzed to this day.

# Hawaiian Note

It wasn't until I stepped on the Hawaiian soil to attend the 1978 Hawaii's Ethnic American Writers' Conference, Talk Story, that I recalled again my father's interlude in Hawaii. Had he not crossed the Pacific from the Hawaiian sugar plantation to San Francisco in the late 1800s, I would have been born Hawaiian.

In my early boyhood days in San Leandro, I used to listen in awe as my father talked Kanaka to his Hawaiian friends. In fact, he spoke better Kanaka than English and appeared to communicate easier his feelings. Naturally, as I was now actually in Hawaii, I began to anticipate emotions and felt akin to the people of the islands.

More than her spectacular scenery, I was intrigued with individuals of various nationalities, talking, listening and learning something one cannot acquire through textbooks. For one example, I met two Hawaiian sisters in their early forties who gave me historical facts that are not stressed in history books. Both the younger sister who is married to an Asian American and the elder one married to an European agreed, "Before you Asians and Europeans migrated to Hawaii, we the so-called native Hawaiians too were immigrants. We too came from other islands in the Pacific and that is why we have so many dialects."

"Why did your ancestors come here when other Pacific islands were just as pleasant?" I said.

One of the sisters smiled and said, "I believe our people fled from oppression; some became stranded here and remained; others desired adventure or sought new opportunities."

141

I nodded in assent because her reply could well explain our Asian forefathers' reasons.

"Now when our relatives get together for a party, it's like an United Nations' conference," said the older sister.

"We have mixed blood of eight nationalities," said the younger one.

During the week of Talk Story Writers' Conference, the most interesting characters were the individuals of multi-lingual background. What astounded me were the economic inroads such as young salesclerks quoting effortlessly sales price in yen to Japanese tourists from Japan. Here I was ignorant of yen exchange. Food of various continents' influence, the islanders blend simply as part of Hawaiian Luau.

As I sat listening to the Conference's keynote speaker calling all young and old Hawaiian writers to write the "great Hawaiian novel," I thought of my early years full of hope and energy and wished I were young again. I envied those who had their whole lives before them— to try and reach their potential.

Everywhere I went, from the humble to the proud, from the poor to the rich, I was entranced with the characters of the island. From a writer's habit, I kept seeking for future materials. I sought life's most precious contribution—male and female living out their lives.

For me in Hawaii there live two of the most outstanding and rare personalities whose lives are engraved in me as long as I am living. One is a Zen priest, T., whom I met but twice. On the first encounter in San Francisco, our eyes met and recognized our identity and felt as if we had known each other all our lives. To me he was the humblest man I had ever met but I had told him, without hesitation, "You are the most evil of men. You know more evil than anyone I know."

He looked at me and smiled.

The other character in Hawaii I know goes beyond gender. A.M., Hawaiian Nisei, is limited of schooling but learned from much suffering. Her steady, piercing eyes tell me much, and I need very little conversation from her to understand and communicate. We are conscious that we are members of a group who translate with a wordless language.

With this note on Hawaii, I must still have time to write the happenings of my father in his early days in Hawaii.

Toshio Mori
*May 1979*